Rohit Patel looked up from th▯ ▯ ▯ ▯ ▯ ▯ing on his laptop was gett▯ ▯ ▯ ▯ ▯ ▯ ▯ ▯ ▯ ▯ feeds all showed much the same thing—it was raining a lot, and where it rained, panic followed. There was something in the rain, something that burrowed and took hold and itched.

He didn't have to watch the news to know that fact—all he had to do was look out the window. He sat in the third-floor laboratory in the main building of Memorial University, looking out over what had been an expanse of lawn sweeping down to the pond. Where, in late April, there should be green shoots and new growth, there was a series of overlapping circles— brown and dark. They hadn't been there earlier that morning. The brown areas looked dead. Rohit knew better.

He looked down the microscope again. The mycelia had grown almost twofold just in the time it had taken him to look up then back again. He had only taken the sample that morning, waiting until the rain stopped, but he already knew more than most of the pundits on the news.

It's definitely fungal. And it's voracious.

The thing he did not know was where it had appeared from all of a sudden. Since his first look at the sample, he'd studied all the known taxonomical texts and databases—and come up with nothing. Yes, it was fungal, but it seemed to be a totally new species that had sprung up out of nowhere, its spores falling in the rain all across the planet.

And everywhere they fall, chaos follows.

FUNGOID

BY WILLIAM MEIKLE

This one is dedicated to firemen everywhere

1

"Just my luck," Jim Noble muttered.

The call came in a minute before he was due to clock off from night shift. Kerry and Stapleton were already on board, so he was probably within his rights to just stroll down the gangway and leave them to it—it wouldn't be the first time. But he'd had a quiet night with no alerts and had even managed a snooze during the hockey replays. He decided to stay and help out where he could; it sounded big—and bad.

As the rapid response team for the busy port of St. John's they mostly dealt with fuel spillage clear-ups, either in the harbor or just off shore, but this time they were called for down in Water Street, in the heart of the old town itself. And as Jim left the radio room he heard the sound of chaos plain enough—sirens in the wind, far too many sirens.

Kerry and Stapleton passed him on the stairs. They were still pulling on their suits so Noble had time to head for his locker and get himself kitted-up. It only took him a few seconds, and by the time he got into the suit and down the gangway their truck was out of the ferry deck and waiting for him on the dockside. He climbed in beside the other two, sliding into his allotted seat, as comfortable as if he were in his old armchair at home, it having been shaped to his rear these past four years now.

Kerry put on the lights and siren, adding to the growing clamor. It wasn't far to their destination—only a couple of hundred yards—but it sounded like they were needed sooner rather than later.

"Fire, do you think?" Stapleton asked as they pulled off the

dock and immediately hit a wall of traffic that was none too
happy at being brought to a complete standstill. All the lights
along the street were green but nobody was moving. They tried
to inch their way slowly past cars and trucks that moved aside,
reluctantly, to allow the truck through. Despite the lights and
siren, it was still slow going.

"Maybe a fire," Jim replied, but there was no plume of smoke
in the sky ahead of them. He could now see the flashing lights
of the police responders at the end of the street, and hear the
faint whine of ambulance sirens—several of them. "Whatever
it is, it's big."

It seemed that the rest of the traffic finally realized it too, at
least the vehicles nearest the scene itself, for the path suddenly
cleared ahead of them and they were able to pull up alongside
the ambulances several seconds later, parking amid a scene of
chaos.

They were outside the town's main bank, and there was a
pickup embedded in the front of it. The bright red truck had
gone off the road, across the concourse, through a large plate
glass window—and it looked like it hadn't slowed at any point
on the way. Three bodies lay on the ground. Relief workers
scurried around, stemming blood, applying bandages and
organizing stretchers, but it didn't look too good for any of the
wounded as far as Jim could tell from a quick glimpse as they
got out of their truck.

Tom Morrison, a local cop that Jim knew to speak to, stood
outside the bank entrance. He looked pale, and green about the
gills—and this was a man that Jim knew had seen more than his
share of drunk-driving accidents and the resulting carnage. Just
seeing the look on the man's face made Jim think he might have
been better off going home when he'd had the chance.

"What is it?" Jim asked. "Did the pickup have something on
board?"

"You could say that," Morrison replied. "We're waiting for
you to tell us. Nobody's ever seen anything like it."

"Spillage?" Jim asked.

"No, at least not yet; it might not even be anything you can
help with. But nobody seems to know what else to do right now.

Best if you take a look for yourself. I hope you didn't have a big breakfast."

Kerry stayed with the truck, and Ted Stapleton joined Jim as they picked their way carefully through the broken glass and bits of the pickup's bodywork to the front end of the truck. It was buried in the bank's main counter, a mangled mess of fender, grille, countertop and cash—a couple hundred dollars' worth of bills by the look of it, all now liberally doused in brake fluid and oil. But that wasn't any more spillage than your normal fender bender, and it wasn't what the team had been called out to see.

The impact had forced much of the engine back through into the driver's seat, and the man—at least Jim thought it had been a man—had his chest caved in by what remained of the steering wheel and column. Several shards of bone pierced both flesh and clothing; it looked like the rib cage had almost exploded on impact, but the bone wasn't white, it was a dull, muddy color. It looked ridged and pitted—almost acid-etched. The force of the collision had been such that the seat belt hadn't saved the driver much injury—at the same time as his chest was being caved in, his face was going in the other direction, into the windshield. Flaps of bloody skin hung from a strangely flattened skull that had been nearly stripped of flesh. There was surprisingly little blood, and what there was looked too watery, too thin—not red but almost brown.

Finally Jim saw why they'd been called out.

The only bit of exposed skin visible—the back of the driver's left hand and some of his forearm—was spotted in tiny red sores, like a bad case of chickenpox that had been scratched, violently, until it bled.

What the hell happened here?

The cop, Morrison, had been right about one thing: it wasn't anything Jim had seen before. Stapleton stepped back sharply, not taking his eyes off the dead man's exposed skin.

"That's not the result of any spillage I know of. Is it some kind of disease?" he whispered. "Tropical maybe?"

"Might be," Jim replied, a chill settling in his spine. "Let's get this area secure—and get everybody back, right back. Find out if anybody touched anything in here, and get them isolated and hosed down. Once we're done inside, we'll hose down the street too. And call the hospital—we need some specialists down here—and we need them fast."

The next twenty minutes were hectic, but all the responders knew their roles, and were good at them. The ambulance staff kept working on the injured. One was dead, two badly hurt, but not fatally so—at least not yet. By rights they should have been on their way to the hospital, but Jim wanted to wait; he was watching for an outbreak of those red spots. They had him worried.

The police got the street cordoned off—much to the displeasure of some of the drivers who had been stuck in the traffic standstill. Jim, Stapleton and Kerry stayed suited up in full hazmat gear. While they waited for the medical specialists, they hosed down as much of the immediate area as they were able with their cocktail of dispersant and disinfectant.

I hope it's enough, thought Jim.

His hope turned to worry when the team arrived from the hospital. He stayed outside the bank as they looked over the body, but he didn't have to hear them to know it was bad—he saw it in the looks on their faces, in the whispered conversations they were having, careful not to be overheard.

If it's that bad, we need to know about it—and we need to know now.

He walked inside.

"Anything you want to tell us poor working stiffs, Docs," Jim said, hearing his voice echo slightly back at him through the mask—he was glad that he'd decided to keep it firmly in place for the meantime.

One of the doctors took Jim to one side and whispered, almost conspiratorially.

"This is the fourth case we've seen since this morning," he said. Jim saw real fear in the man's eyes, and felt it grow inside him too. "Mount Pearl, Paradise, and an accident in Airport Heights. It's already all over town—and we have no idea what it is or how to deal with it."

As Jim walked back out onto the concourse he felt the patter of raindrops on his suit.

The screaming started seconds later.

2

Mycelium is the vegetative part of a fungus, consisting of a mass of branching, thread-like hyphae. The mass of hyphae is sometimes called shiro, especially within the fairy ring fungi. Fungal colonies composed of mycelium are found in and on soil and many other substrates. A typical single spore germinates into a homokaryotic mycelium. A mycelium may be minute, forming a colony that is too small to see, or it may be extensive.

Through the mycelium, a fungus absorbs nutrients from its environment. It does this in a two-stage process. First, the hyphae secrete enzymes onto or into the food source, which break down biological polymers into smaller units such as monomers. These monomers are then absorbed into the mycelium by facilitated diffusion and active transport.

A honey fungus with a mycelial spread measuring 2.4 miles across in the Blue Mountains in Oregon is thought to be the largest living organism on Earth.

It started to rain just as Rebecca Lovatt drove down into the underground garage beneath the mall, heavy spatters that seemed somewhat oily and smeared themselves across the glass when she deployed the wipers. There was still a greasy streak there when she reached Level Three and pulled into a parking space, a streak that was proving too difficult to dispel, even with two squirts of the heavy-duty wash. She was in too much of a hurry to take a closer look; she had a bunch of other chores to do before the kids needed picking up, and there was just enough time for her to pick up Shaun's birthday present.

The gift—a silver pocket watch and chain that Shaun had admired on his last trip home—cost more than she'd have liked, but he would be back with the family next week and she wanted things to be just right. It had been a long contract—three months apart, the longest since they met—and she couldn't wait to see him, to hand over the small box and see his face light up.

That was what she was thinking about when she got to the shop, so she missed some of the start of what the young girl behind the jeweler's counter was saying—something about a big accident downtown.

"They say it's a bad one," the girl continued. "Water Street's closed off and the traffic's snarled up all along Duckworth Street and up past the Fairmont. I was supposed to be getting my hair done at Josie's when I get off and ..."

Rebecca tried to nod in the right places. She was now busy checking that the pocket watch was the one she'd ordered, and only had half her attention on the one-sided conversation. The girl didn't seem too worried—she seemed the sort that liked to hear herself speak to remind herself she was still a person, and not some robotic mannequin behind a counter. Rebecca let her ramble on—she was onto her boyfriend now, and what a waste of space he was—but at least she'd started to process the payment while berating the lad. Rebecca already felt sorry for him, and she'd never met him.

She paid up and left the small jewelry shop on the main drag of the mall, intending to go straight back down to the parking lot. She was so intent on ensuring she got the watch securely tucked away deep in her purse that she didn't notice until she was almost on top of it that there was a commotion near the main doorway. A small crowd gathered, peering out to the roadway beyond. She saw thick black smoke rising outside, through the glass over their heads.

Another accident?

Then she heard the screams, high and wild as if someone was being tortured, scarily loud even through the closed doors. Another scream joined the first, then another. Two people peeled off the watching group by the door and headed off in the direction of the parking garage escalator. Rebecca slid quickly into one of the vacated spaces, and got a first look out.

She saw the burning cars first—two of them in what had obviously been a head-on collision. A body lay half-fallen out of the driver's door of the nearest vehicle. The woman's hands waved feebly—but no one was moving to help. There were already cops on the scene—three of them—but instead of helping the woman they stood at one side, scratching wildly at their hands, their heads, their arms, raising red welts and streams of blood that ran in rivulets in a steady wash of rain.

"Help them," someone near Rebecca said. "We need to help them."

But nobody moved—they all stood there, silent, watching the cops scratch and scream, all of them unable to process what they were seeing. Rebecca looked past the crash scene, across the mall's outdoor parking bays. There were more people there, and like the cops they too scratched and thrashed, as if the rain was attacking them in some way.

Rebecca remembered the oily smear she'd left on the windshield.

Then she remembered the kids.

She turned and ran for the escalator.

On reaching Level Three she had to step back quickly as a speeding pickup, engine revving wildly, tore past her, scraped heavily along the restraining wall, and bounced rather than drove up out of the garage. Somewhere nearby someone wept piteously, but Rebecca felt no compulsion to stop and check. Her only thought was for the kids—Adam and Mark—and the idea, too big for her head, that they might have been outside in the schoolyard playing when the rain came.

It took her three tries to get the key in the ignition, her hands shaking. Finally she got it, and almost hit the sedan opposite as she came out of the parking space too fast. She got the turn under control just in time and circled up and out of the garage as fast as she was able, trying not to look at the greasy streak that ran down the windshield right in front of her.

Just as she came up the last ramp out of the mall someone,

blood pouring down their face as they tore chunks of hair from their scalp, almost stumbled right in front of her, forcing her to brake hard. The man—that was only obvious when he took his hands away from his face—seemed oblivious to her at first, but when she tried to drive on, he slapped his palms, hard, on the hood of her SUV and yelled something incoherent before staggering away. Rebecca saw him in the rear-view mirror, hunched over and tearing at his scalp, then he was lost from sight as she drove out into the large open area to the rear of the mall.

The junction out into the main road was blocked—another accident—and she had to turn left when she wanted to go right. Even then, two bodies writhed on the ground in the middle of the road—more blood, more frantic scratching—and she had to swerve to avoid running over them.

Spots of rain splattered on the windshield, leaving more greasy marks when the wipers swept over them. She could hear the rain drum on the roof of the SUV—and again she thought of the kids, and the rain hitting them on their heads, their arms. She had to swerve to avoid three more people; their distress was obvious, the blood even more so. But she wouldn't, couldn't, stop.

Adam. Mark. I'm coming.

She couldn't dare to take her eyes off the road to rummage for her phone—besides, she'd be there almost as quickly as she could make a call—but everywhere she looked she saw more blood, more frenzied people in obvious pain.

What the hell is going on here?

She wasn't made any the wiser on the short drive down the loop to the school—it was something in the rain, that much was obvious—something that caused anyone exposed to it tear and scratch at their skin and scalps.

Acid? Rebecca thought. *Is this a chemical accident?*

Another thought struck her—a worse one.

Is this a terrorist attack?

She drove wildly, foot down full on the accelerator. Luckily traffic was light. There was another accident on the corner of Watson and French, and she saw the drivers, both hunched over their wheels, unmoving. But there was no sign of any respond-ers—no cops, no ambulance, and Rebecca herself was in no mood to stop. It took her a while to notice that she seemed to have driven out of the spattering rain. The loop took her down to the foot of the hill below Watson Drive and as she turned into the schoolyard she saw that the rain cloud hung, black and heavy, over the most elevated part of town. Even now sweep-ing tendrils of gray were reaching further down the hill; they looked to be almost alive.

Two other cars screeched into the schoolyard just behind her. She recognized one of the women, Patty Payne, whose daughter Annie was in Mark's grade. The other was a redhead she hadn't seen before, but all three of them got out of the vehi-cles together, one determined unit as they went through the school door.

A burly guard immediately tried to stop them. Rebecca noticed he had a crowd pacifier on his hip—he hadn't reached for it yet, but there was something in his eyes that told her he might, if pressed.

"Can I help you, ladies?"

Rebecca tried to keep her voice calm.

"I would like to take my boys—Adam and Mark Lovatt—home, please."

"We will need a good reason for that," the guard said.

"How about acid fucking rain killing folks in the street," the redhead said, and started to try to push past the man, scream-ing. "Ira Kaminski—get your ass out here, right now."

"Madam," the guard said, trying to hold the woman back. "If you don't calm down I'll have to call the police."

"Go ahead and try," the woman replied. "They won't come—they've got bigger things on their mind."

Rebecca saw confusion in the man's eyes, and worked on it quickly while they had an opportunity.

"Just come to the door and look out," she said softly. "You'll see what we mean."

The redhead took her chance and ran off down the corridor, screaming for her Ira. The guard wanted to follow, but by this time Rebecca was on one side of him, Patty on the other, taking him by the arm and leading his to the main door.

The rain was closer now, more than halfway down the hill. The cloud hung low over the upper part of town—but not low enough to obscure the small clusters of flames and smoke that rose from several places.

"What happened?"

"We have no idea," Rebecca said. "But we're taking our kids."

The guard opened the door. Screams came in the air from up the hill—wailing, tortured screams.

"We're taking our kids," Patty echoed softly, and Rebecca joined her in heading off along the corridor. The guard let them go, unable to take his eyes off the scene outside.

They found Mark and Annie first. The kids were all at the main window of their room, overlooking the town, and when Mark turned at her call she saw the same confusion and fear she felt inside her.

"Where's Adam?"

"3B—two doors down," Mark replied.

By the time she'd fetched Adam—not without a yelling match with a young teacher who looked more frightened than any of the kids, the light in the school had definitely grown dimmer—the rain cloud was sweeping down the hill, moving almost overhead.

"Time to go," Patty Payne said, and as a group all five of them ran back towards the entrance. The redhead and her Ira were already there, although the guard blocked the route back out to the vehicles.

"Look, I can see you're worried—but it might be dangerous out there," he said. "The kids could be hurt."

"That's why we're taking them home."

"What about the others here?"

"Keep them inside—they'll be safe inside," Patty said, although Rebecca was by no means sure that was going to be the case—she just wanted to be home, needed to be home. She saw past the guard out the door. It was getting very dark out there now, and rain wasn't far away.

"We're going. When the rain starts, don't let any hit you. Trust us on this."

The guard put a hand on the pacifier, then thought better of it and stood aside.

"Okay. Just promise me you'll be careful, and make sure they're here with a note tomorrow."

Rebecca almost laughed. She had a feeling that notes were quickly going to be least of the man's worries, but she had no time for any chat, and she shepherded the kids outside. The kids were confused, and more than a bit excited at being out of school so early. They immediately ran across the play area.

"Get your asses back here," Rebecca shouted. "Right fucking now."

She saw both Annie's shocked, wide-eyed expression, and Patty's barely suppressed grin, but it had done the job. It was the first time she'd ever sworn in front of the boys; she only hoped she'd get a chance to do it again. She had to yell again—no swearing this time—to get them to climb up into the SUV, and she was nearly too late. She saw two raindrops pitter-patter on the roof as she got into the driver's seat.

Patty hadn't been as quick. Annie was in the passenger seat and Patty stood outside the car, bent over and fiddling with the tension of her seat belt. She yelped in pain, like the bark of a small dog; Rebecca heard it clearly. Patty scratched at her hand even as she threw herself into the car and slammed the door, hard, behind her.

The redhead and her Ira were already headed off across the yard at speed as heavier rain started to spatter on the windshield—more grease that the wipers couldn't quite deal with. Rebecca drove over and put the SUV up next to Patty's car before slightly lowering the driver's-side window, checking that no rain was going to get in before lowering it further.

"You okay, Patty?"

The other woman smiled, grimaced, and showed Rebecca a fresh red weal on the back of her hand.

"It was a little black speck of something. It hurt like a steam-iron burn at first, but as soon as I scraped it off it was fine. Just don't get any of that shit on you."

Patty would normally wash her mouth out with carbolic soap rather than let a cuss word pass her lips.

Looks like there's a first time for everything for both of us today.

"I hear you," Rebecca said. "Call me if you need anything, okay?"

Patty nodded, and they both drove off, parting company at Watson and French—the accident was still there, as were the bodies in the drivers' seats. The boys' eyes went wide in astonishment but neither they nor Rebecca said anything as they drove past without stopping.

The black rain spattered huge oily drops on the windshield, drops that the wipers smeared across Rebecca's vision until the world beyond was misty and almost opaque.

She drove home on autopilot; luckily there was no traffic, although they passed half a dozen more accidents. More worrying, there were no responders at any of them—no police, ambulance or fire workers to be seen.

What the hell is going on here?

3

Shaun Lovatt was thinking the same thing at the same time on the other side of the country, on a forest trail in Alberta. The Caterpillar plow that served as their primary mode of transport in the spring was taking them up to the high lumber working area. But where the foliage should be verdant and deep green there were only brown, withered branches, dank gray lichen and a pervading stench of rot; it was so bad that they had to close the windows.

"What the hell is this? Some kind of blight?"

He turned to Joe in the passenger seat—the big man didn't speak and couldn't take his eyes from the view, as if he didn't believe what he saw.

"I was up here last Friday, Shaun," he finally said. "There's no blight will do this in a week. If you ask me, this is chemical—a spill maybe? Something jettisoned from a plane?"

"We'd have heard of something this bad, surely?"

"We haven't heard much of anything—that's why we're here, remember?"

They'd been trying to reach the logging camp on the radio for nearly two days now with no reply forthcoming. Four long flatbed trucks had gone up the hill, but no timber, no trucks—and no one—had come back down. It happened occasionally here in the Alberta Rockies—camps sometimes got cut off, usually due to a burst of inclement weather—but apart from heavy rain on the highest land last weekend it had been mostly fair. There was hardly even any snow left on the ground, and the plow was making good time up the slopes.

But Shaun was starting to worry just what it was they were heading into.

They rolled into the camp twenty minutes later. Shaun wasn't expecting a reception committee—this was a working camp after all. But he was expecting some activity, some sign that work was underway, or at least had been recently. Nothing moved. The whole site sat in thin fog, but not anything that would cause any delay. There was big money in timber, and big money meant quick turnarounds and continual deliveries of logs off the slopes. Whatever was going on here now, it certainly wasn't making the company any money.

The main site was little more than a wide, cleared area of recent and old sawdust, pine needles and stumps, with the four long flatbeds parked neatly in one corner and three log cabins at the far end. There should at least have been smoke from the chimneys but there was none. When Shaun killed the plow's engine and rolled down his window, just an inch, he remembered the smell. They were met with deathly silence punctuated only by the sound of moisture dripping from the dead, brown branches of the trees. Indeed, whatever was causing the die-off seemed even worse up here. All of the trees in the area had been stripped clean of any needles and there was not a single hint of greenery to be seen. Even the undergrowth—normally lush with ferns—had taken on the same brown tone, and when Shaun opened the plow door the stench of rot got so pungent that he closed it again immediately and sat back in his seat.

"It wasn't me—it was the dog," Joe said, and smiled thinly. "If there's anybody around, they'll be in the mess room. Drive over to the door, would you? I'm not keen on walking too far out there."

"I hear you, brother," Shaun replied. He drove the plow over to park right up next to the door of the nearest cabin. The noise should have been more than enough to bring somebody running, but the whole site was still silent when he cut the engine again.

Joe, on the passenger side, was nearest the doorway.

"After you," Shaun said. The big man covered his mouth with a hand, gave Shaun the okay sign, and left in a hurry.

Shaun waited for a further sign that he should join him.

The only sound now was the ticking and metallic clangs of the plow engine as it started to cool.

He should be back by now.

Still Shaun waited. He knew from experience that any stupidity, any hasty action up on these mountains could get you dead quickly. He drummed his gloved hands on the steering wheel, then stopped—although little more than a dull thud, the noise seemed too loud, too out of place in what was starting to feel like a burial ground more than a work site.

Come on, Joe. What's keeping you?

At that same moment, Joe came back into the doorway. All the color had drained from his face, and he looked like he'd just thrown up his breakfast. He waved for Shaun to join him. Shaun remembered to cover his mouth before opening the door and climbing down out of the plow's cab. Out in the open it felt even more like a cemetery as nothing moved—no wind, no sound, not even a bird cry or rustle of branches. The stench was almost unbearable, burning at his nostrils like diesel fumes, and once again he thought of Joe's theory of some kind of chemical spillage.

Joe stood aside and motioned that Shaun should go past him into the cabin.

"You need to see this—we're both going to need to be telling the same story. They won't believe it if it comes from just one of us."

The big man wouldn't say any more, and showed little inclination to return into the cabin. Shaun stepped past him and entered the main room.

At least the smell of rot wasn't so bad in here, but that didn't make up for the sight of the bodies that lay strewn around the room—in seats, on the floor and, bizarrely, laid out on the long trestle table. He had a closer look at the one on the table first, and quickly wished he hadn't. It was Bert, the foreman—the gray in the beard gave it away, but it was really the only bit of the man still recognizable. The rest was dried out and sunken—*mummified* was the word that came to mind first, although the exposed skin had the same brown tone that Shaun had got used to seeing on the trees and ground on the way up the slope. Whatever had gotten to the vegetation, it seemed it had got to the men too.

He did a quick headcount. Eleven bodies.

There should be twelve of them—eight of ours and four truck drivers.

There wasn't much else for him to see. A large pot of congealed stew sat on the stove, but he couldn't get close enough to investigate—it stank as bad as anything outside. As far as he could tell there was no indication as to how the men had died, beyond the dry brown skin, and Shaun wasn't about to inspect that any closer than he had to.

He went back out onto the doorstep. Joe handed him a freshly lit smoke.

"I quit, remember?" Shaun started, then the stench hit again. He took the cigarette and had a long draw.

"It helps," Joe said. "Trust me. Today's not a good day to stay on the wagon."

Shaun sucked smoke for several seconds. It did indeed help with the stench, although it was still there, still almost overpowering.

"There are eleven in there," he said. "Maybe there's still someone alive up here?"

Joe pointed over at the four long flatbeds. The door to the nearest was open. Just below it, on the ground, was a dried-out, brown mound. It could have been just leaf mold and litter, but Shaun was pretty sure they'd found the last body.

"Now what?" he said.

Joe stubbed out his smoke.

"We should check the other cabins, just to make sure. And use the radio to call this in, although as I said, we both need to have our story straight—this is going to take some telling."

"I can tell you something for nothing. I'm none too happy at hanging around any longer than we have to."

"You and me both," Joe replied. "Just a quick check of the other cabins, a radio call, then we can be off down the hill and let somebody else clear up."

To save on time they took a cabin each. Shaun got the bunks; in some ways he was glad that all the bodies were already accounted for, because he didn't think he could have coped with seeing any more brown mummies laid out in the cots. The cabin was bare and empty save for the paraphernalia of day-to-day living up here—shavers, combs, duffel bags, damp socks and rucksacks, the domesticity in stark contrast to the horrors next door in the mess.

Almost absent-mindedly, Shaun bent to pick a discarded sock off the floor. It would not lift—it was stuck hard to a rug, which was in turn stuck hard to the wooden flooring. He bent closer and saw that the wool of the sock and the weave of the rug were intertwined and meshed together—like some kind of natural Velcro, something that looked oily, and brown.

Without even realizing it, he was out on the doorstep again, gulping in air and fighting hard to keep down a rising sense of panic. Joe called out from the third cabin.

"In here, Shaun. One more thing you need to see with me."

The third cabin served as the office and admin area for the work crew—two laptops, a printer, a coffee pot, and a couple of chairs around a trestle. But the thing Joe needed him to see was the radio set.

"Did you get through?" Shaun asked.

Joe just laughed bitterly.

"I don't even want to touch it."

Joe saw what the big man meant when he had a look for himself. It was more of the brown, oily tendrils, a mass of them all across the microphone and the dials, and creeping up the face of the radio. Below that, on the glass of two of the display panels, were smears of something more recognizable—the red, just starting to brown, of drying blood.

"What the fuck happened here?" Shaun whispered.

"I don't have a clue," Joe replied, "but I think it's still happening. I vote we get the hell out of Dodge before it gets us too."

Shaun wasn't about to disagree. He headed out for the plow. Joe held back.

"Get the engine running. I just want to get the log book. There might be something in there that'll tell us what happened."

Shaun had just got inside and switched on the engine when heavy, oily raindrops started to spatter against the plow's windshield. Joe stepped out of the cabin and immediately threw a hand to his head as if he'd been stung. He yelped again as he pulled himself up into the passenger seat and pulled the door shut. He dropped the log book on the floor at his feet and scratched frantically at his scalp, then at the back of his hand, raising a welt and a line of thin, watery blood.

"Bloody hell, that smarts," the big man said. "There's something in the rain—acid maybe?" He kept scratching at his head as he turned to Shaun. "This is not good. Get us the hell out of here."

They got back down the hill in half the time it had taken them to go up. Shaun smoked another of Joe's Camels—his first cigarettes for more than nine years, but Becky would forgive him, just this once. And thinking of Becky and the boys made him drive ever faster, throwing the plow down the hill track and taking too many risks on too many corners. Normally that would have earned him a ticking-off from Joe, but the big man wasn't paying much attention, alternating between looking at the log book and scratching frantically at his scalp.

"It itches like fucking crazy," was all that he would say. "Just get us off this hill—we need somebody to have a good look at it."

Shaun saw fear in the big man's eyes. They were thinking the same thing: brown, oily tendrils, creeping through wool and carpet, through blood and tissue.

What the hell is going on here?

4

Rohit Patel looked up from the microscope—the news streaming on his laptop was getting too insistent to ignore. The feeds all showed much the same thing—it was raining a lot, and where it rained, panic followed. There was something in the rain, something that burrowed and took hold and itched.

And fed.

It's worldwide.

We're in serious trouble.

He didn't have to watch the news to know that fact—all he had to do was look out the window. He sat in the third-floor laboratory in the main building of Memorial University, looking out over what had been an expanse of lawn sweeping down to the pond. Where, in late April, there should be green shoots and new growth, there was a series of overlapping circles— brown and dark. They hadn't been there earlier that morning. The brown areas looked dead. Rohit knew better.

He looked down the microscope again. The mycelia had grown almost twofold just in the time it had taken him to look up then back again. He had only taken the sample that morning, waiting until the rain stopped, but he already knew more than most of the pundits on the news.

It's definitely fungal. And it's voracious.

The thing he did not know was where it had appeared from all of a sudden. Since his first look at the sample, he'd studied all the known taxonomical texts and databases—and come up with nothing. Yes, it was fungal, but it seemed to be a totally new species that had sprung up out of nowhere, its spores falling in the rain all across the planet.

And everywhere they fall, chaos follows.

After the panic in the rain shower that morning, St. John's had settled into an uneasy quiet. From the window Rohit had a good view of the ring road, which was almost devoid of traffic—something previously unheard of at this time of day. There were no students walking in the grounds, and in the far distance the section of the Trans-Canada Highway that stretched away to the west was equally deserted. Rohit could almost believe he had somehow slept through a day without noticing and it was now early Sunday morning.

But then there were the new reports, the most terrifying of which were from the Far East. Vast swathes of forest had gone brown almost overnight, the tracking helicopter shots showing mile after mile of vegetation overrun by the same mycelia that Rohit had on his slide. And as if that wasn't bad enough, rioting and looting had broken out in the Philippines, Taiwan and Hong Kong as a tropical storm lashed them with rain that brought down a flood of burrowing spores on the unwary.

Glasgow in Scotland had gone offline earlier that morning after a rainstorm, and it was currently raining down spores in Paris, Bucharest and Vancouver. South of the Equator, the situation seemed less dire, although Rohit had already heard a rumor that a vast tract of the Amazon rainforest was currently going brown and that no one knew the cause.

There was one other news item of note, and Rohit was starting to worry that it was the most important story of them all. Amid all the stories of panic and disorder that fueled the news frenzy, there was a smaller item that was not getting much attention. The Chinese had let off a nuclear explosion—some said test—in a remote part of Mongolia. But Rohit knew it wasn't quite as remote as they were making out. Xanhai province was known for its high desert—and for the laboratories, where the Chinese performed their chemical research. They'd sounded him out for a position at one of the sites, two years back; a mycologist or fungal specialist with experience in the food industry was the job description.

He looked at the news, then back down the scope at what he had on his slide. He had a horrible sick feeling in the pit of his stomach that the Chinese had been working on something completely new.

And they've let it escape.

Normally Rohit could spend hours alone in the lab, lost in the minutiae of his research. Some days he would be the only one in the building and it had never bothered him—until now. Now there was a sense of impending doom, a sword hanging overhead just about to fall, and Rohit felt the need for company—any company, just as long as he wasn't alone with his fears for what might happen in the coming days.

He stood from the scope, had one last look at the news reports—rain, terrible rain, in Berlin now—and headed downstairs to the cafeteria.

Coffee, and plenty of it.

On arriving at the ground floor he was once again struck by the almost cathedral-like quiet and emptiness of the area. It did not feel like term time at all and he assumed that the morning's rains, and subsequent panic, had led most staff and students to make a run for family and home.

Rohit had neither—not here in this town, nor anywhere else on the suddenly panicked planet. He could walk across campus to the flat they had provided for his tenure, hunker down in the block there with his empty refrigerator and bad television reception—or he could stay in the lab, with Wi-Fi, free coffee, and a certain sense of security.

Not a difficult choice at all under the circumstances.

There were only two tables occupied, both in the nook near the television set. There were two distinct groups of students of about a dozen each, one group animated, almost excited, the other dejected and morose. Rohit wasn't in the mood to converse with either. He went to the counter and ordered a tall coffee.

"There's no muffin this morning, sir," the always cheery woman behind the counter said. "No deliveries, see, what with the trouble and all."

She waved a hand towards the nook and the television.

"Terrible times. But I'm sure it'll all be under control soon."

She looked at Rohit as if expecting confirmation—he'd seen

that look before. As a scientist he was often expected to have magic answers available at the drop of a hat. And sometimes he had them.

But not today.

He took his coffee and turned away before he would have to see the disappointment, and worry, in the woman's eyes.

He still wasn't ready to go back to the lab. The sound of chattering students was just enough to remind him of normal days, quiet days spent in research—the reason he was here at all. But seeing the pictures coming through on the television, he thought that those kinds of days might be few and far between, in the near future at least.

The main Canadian news channel was switching rapidly between stories, trying—and mostly failing—to keep up with the pace of the breaking news. At the moment they showed a scene of a helicopter flying over the grain fields of the American Midwest— what was left of them anyway. The brown circles—identical to the ones Rohit had seen on the lawn outside his lab window—covered the ground like some vast crop circle hoax. Only this was clearly no hoax. The scale of it, covering thousands of square miles, was almost too big to comprehend.

The scene switched from rural to city. Rohit recognized the view immediately, as he'd walked it many times as a student himself—London, and the grand parade down the mall from Trafalgar Square to Buckingham Palace. Only now it wasn't quite so grand—the avenue of willow, sycamore and chestnut trees, so splendid in their prime, were now rotted, brown skeletal ruins. The camera, affixed to a motorbike by the look of it, zoomed in at the base of one of the trees. The resident pelicans of St James' Park were famous for eating anything that came close to them—sandwiches, hot dogs, rats and even pigeons. But now two of them had befallen a similar fate themselves. They lay mostly buried under a mass of twisted brown fibers that crept and crawled over and through the large birds.

"Ugh. Gross," a voice said from the nearest occupied table, but Rohit couldn't take his eyes from the still mounds of dead birds as the camera zoomed in closer to show the mycelia reaching down the birds' gullets, heading deeper in search of the softer parts.

It's not just consuming vegetation. It's eating flesh too.

As he took what remained of the coffee back up to his lab, there was only one thought at the front of his mind.

We're in really serious trouble.

5

Jim Noble's day went to hell fast. He'd thought the rain shower downtown at the initial crash scene was the worst thing he'd ever see. He'd never forget the sudden panic in the streets, nor the immediate aftermath when they had to hose down the dead and dying while the screaming went on around them, not knowing what was going on, knowing only that he had to try to contain it.

But that rain had only been a quick shower, affecting a score of people in a small area, and they'd thought they had things under control—for all of five minutes. It was even almost calm, until someone turned up who'd been watching the news, and someone else mentioned more rain up near the airport, and another call came in, then another. It was raining in spots all over town. People were dying all over town. Anything Jim's team could do about it was going to be far too little, far too late.

When he finally found a moment where he could stop spraying and draw a breath, Jim looked for Morrison, but the cop was nowhere around.

"Gone to look out for his family," a younger cop said. "He suggested we should all do the same."

Which wouldn't be a bad idea—if I had anybody that gave a fuck.

He saw Stapleton over by the truck—Ted had taken his helmet off, and was in the process of shedding the hazmat suit.

"You heard the cop," the small man said when Jim went over to him. "I've got kids up in Hamilton Park School. And Sarah's at the mall as far as I know. I'm heading up that way—I'll find them."

"Then what?" Jim said softly.

"How the fuck do I know? But I'm not staying here—I know that much. Have you seen the news? The whole planet's going to hell. It's every man for himself."

Stapleton was only the first of many, mostly family men, to cut and run in the first frantic hours. For those who remained it quickly became a matter of containment—after a visit back to the boat for the issue of more hazmat suits, they spent the next few hours getting people to stay indoors. In truth, most of them didn't need much persuasion. They ferried the more badly affected to hospital waiting rooms that were getting quickly overrun with the afflicted. They took the dead—too many dead—to the crematorium, which was already working flat out, and still failing to keep up. The pile of bodies covered only in plastic sheeting was growing and would soon spill over out of the mortuary.

They also started seeing the results of the creep of the brown filaments and the rapid destruction of their town and people. All of the green places were going brown fast, the avenues lined with only dead branches, the air filled with the stench of rot. Jim could only guess at the number of dead—and dying—inside the quiet houses they passed on their rounds.

By late afternoon the decision came down from the town councilmen: quarantine was needed, and needed fast. Jim was assigned to getting unaffected folks to the Delta Hotel; the three taciturn, armed men who went with the cleanup crew were assigned to make sure folks stayed there. He heard over a rushed coffee that there were other crews—less worried about the able, more worried about the infected—and that the words *execution squad* were being bandied about. He didn't want to believe it, but having seen how quickly things were turning to shit, he couldn't disbelieve it either.

But the main thing that ruined Jim's day was intimately more personal than any of that. It happened so fast he almost missed it.

The call came in from the lumberyard at five in the afternoon. Jim was aware he was running on fumes—it had been a long,

long day fueled mainly by coffee and chocolate bars with only a
few snatched periods of what could only loosely be called rest.
A mistake was almost inevitable.

Six of them—three in each truck—rolled into the lumberyard parking lot and immediately found trouble. The yard held
tall stacks of wood—building supplies for most of the town,
piled high around three sides of the parking bay. None of it was
ever going to be used now, for it was clearly riddled with the
brown filaments.

They were tempted to not even get out of the trucks, for
when they cracked open a window to check, the stench of rot
was almost overpowering. But it was also clear that there were
people in the main warehouse. The door had opened at their
approach, and at least two figures stood in the doorway.

Jim went first, got out of the truck, and had already started
to walk over when he saw they had arrived too late. The two
people in the doorway were, like the wood, riddled with infection, so much so that Jim was surprised they were still standing; the brown threads covered most of the bare skin he could
see. And there were more of the infected in the warehouse with
them—half a dozen of them were already coming out into the
yard, with more in the doorway behind them. Jim was aware
that he was caught in no man's land, between the warehouse
door and the trucks behind him. He heard Kerry shout his
name but couldn't afford to turn.

The first two people were only yards away now, their arms
outstretched, as if begging for Jim's help. He saw with dis-
may that they wouldn't answer if he spoke; their mouths were
almost completely filled with brown tissue, and the woman on
the right had already lost one eye to infection and was near to
losing the other.

"I'm sorry," Jim said—it was all he could say—and tried
to back away. They followed, two more joining the others, all
reaching out, all needing help he couldn't give.

The nearest man to him raised an arm higher. Jim saw the
knife too late, and everything that happened in the next two
seconds seemed to take place in slow motion. The knife came
down and sliced into the fabric of the suit at Jim's wrist even as

the man fell aside, his face blown away by gunfire that seemed to come over Jim's shoulder and set the oncoming infected to dancing like puppets in bloody rain.

By the time Jim registered that the knife had cut his suit, it was all over—the infected lay dead at his feet, and Jim didn't even stop to look, but turned at a run for the truck, hosing himself down and trying to find his breath.

Once back in the safety of the cab he slid off his glove and checked his skin. It hadn't been broken, and there was no sign of a red dot. The dispersant and detergent had got through the hole in the suit and left a raw-looking redness at his wrist, but that was all. Jim let out a sigh of relief then put the glove back on and sealed the suit at the sleeve with black rubber tape they kept for emergencies.

When Kerry stepped up into the cab doorway and asked if he was okay, Jim could only nod in reply. It was only after the cleanup crew were finished in the yard that his heart rate slowed and the panic subsided enough for him to step back out and help.

6

Rebecca's day since getting home with the kids had passed in a dazed blur. Adam and Mark were oblivious to the growing panic in the world outside, having spent their time on the sofa shouting insults between themselves as they played the latest game on the big screen. Rebecca had tried to lose her thoughts in domesticity, but laundry and cooking were no substitute for the news that was playing, sound muted, on the tabletop set in the kitchen while she worked.

Now the chores were done and she was sitting, coffee mug in hand, half-watching the mayhem on the news, and half-waiting for the phone to ring. She knew Shaun would be working—probably somewhere remote, probably out of range of a cell signal—but the worry was growing in her with each passing minute, and she needed to hear from him. She'd already tried the number she had for emergencies—the logging company's office in Banff—but all she got was a constant engaged tone.

The light was starting to go as evening came on, and the news got darker too. She lost count of the number of times she saw the close-up of the two dead birds in London, but by late afternoon that was replaced by a new horror—and one too close to home for comfort.

She didn't know London, but she knew Central Park, New York—they had been there on their honeymoon. Now it was a brown, devastated wasteland. But more than that, there were mounds where there should be flat grass—suspiciously human-shaped mounds. This time the camera did not, thankfully, linger too long on the gory details, but the reporter's horror came through loud and clear. Whatever was happening, it was taking people—a lot of people.

And nobody seems to know the cause.

Preparing a supper for the boys grounded her back in something closer to normality—for a while—but after the boys were bathed and bedded she was left with the too-quiet house and the growing scenes of madness on the news.

It was getting bad, fast. Rain fell around the northern hemisphere, and people fell under the crawling chaos of the brown filaments. It was obvious now that this was far more than a localized issue. Some countries had closed their borders and gone quiet, but that only made the situation seem even worse somehow.

Maybe I should leave town—head for somewhere more remote.

But the thought of even venturing outside filled her with dread—at least here on her couch she could pretend the news was far off and far away.

Her phone beeped, causing her to start violently and spill coffee—thankfully gone cold—down her sleeve. She picked up the phone and checked; she had an incoming text message. But she didn't get time to read it.

The porch light went on. Someone was moving around out there.

If that's Debbie Thomas' dog again, I'll have its hide.

She stepped over to the window, catching a glimpse of something pale. It took her a second or two to recognize the girl. Young Annie Payne stood there, crying deep racking sobs.

"I didn't know where else to go," she said as Rebecca opened the door, and that was the last thing she said before falling into a dead faint.

The girl woke as Rebecca carried her inside and laid her on the sofa, covering her with a woolen throw.

"Where's your mum, sweetheart?" Rebecca asked, trying to keep her voice calm and free of the growing nervous worry that was threatening to eat her up from the stomach outward. At first she didn't think the girl would answer, then Annie nodded toward the patio door.

"She got too heavy for me."

"She's out there? Close?"

Annie nodded, and her eyes fluttered, as if she might lapse into unconsciousness again at any moment. Rebecca patted her on the cheek.

"You rest, dear," she said. "I'll see to your mum."

A small hand grabbed Rebecca tight at the wrist.

"It's too late," the girl whispered, then let go.

Rebecca's worry grew even larger, and she had to force her legs to move, to stand and head for the porch. Even then she had enough presence of mind to stop at the doorway and look out, checking for any sign of rain. She saw a crescent moon, and the evening star. The breeze that came in the door felt crisp—late-springtime clear. It seemed safe, for now. She took a last look at the girl on the sofa, who looked to be asleep, then stepped out into the backyard.

In no more than four steps she was beyond the range of the porch light and it took her eyes several seconds to adjust to the gloom beyond. The ground underfoot felt soft, almost soggy, but she couldn't feel any damp rising into her house shoes—if she had she'd have fled back inside in a shot.

"Patty?" she called out softly. She heard traffic in the distance, and a plane went over high up but the houses on either side of theirs sat dark and quiet. She hoped that just meant that her neighbors had been smart enough to stay at work.

"Patty?" she called again, and stepped farther from the safety of the porch light. She was getting used to the gloom now, and saw familiar features—the juniper bush Shaun had planted the day after they moved in, the azalea that came from a cutting from her mum's place, and the row of conifers that would one day be a boundary fence.

If we live long enough to see it.

She pushed that thought from her head.

"Patty?" Despite her obvious seclusion she still couldn't bring herself to raise her voice above a stage whisper. "Are you out here?"

She stopped, still, listening for a reply, or a groan, anything that would tell her the woman was indeed here in the yard, but there was only a silence, one that seemed to get deeper and thicker as Rebecca moved further into the gloom.

She was about to give up and turn for the house when she saw something that shouldn't be there—a low mound on the grass that looked all too familiar from the news reports. And she knew immediately who it must be—the mop of blonde hair was clearly visible despite the dim light.

"Aw, Jesus, Patty—what's happened here?"

She stepped forward, then stopped as she got a close look at what had become of the woman. Patty Payne lay face down in the grass, and she wasn't moving—but something else was, something that seemed to writhe and coil like a nest of tiny worms as it grew in and around the prone woman's flesh.

"Patty?"

But Rebecca could see—far too clearly—that the woman was gone. Her arm was the worst thing; Rebecca remembered seeing the red spot, burned into Patty's hand by the rain, as she got into the car in the schoolyard.

Was that all it took?

Brown filaments had ravaged the flesh, and what had been skin, bone and muscle was now a dried mass of dark tissue seemingly composed of fine threads. Those same threads ran across what Rebecca could see of the woman's face—thankfully her eyes were closed; Rebecca didn't want to see what had become of them. Further down the body Patty's skirt was pulled up, exposing her thighs, the pale flesh almost completely subsumed under more of the writhing brown fibers. Her feet were bare, bloody. There was something else, something Rebecca had to move even closer to see—the brown fibroid tissue covered the soles of the feet in a thick mat, almost carpet like—and they had already started to creep into, and mesh with, the grass of the lawn. For six inches around either foot the vegetation writhed and wafted despite the lack of a wind—swaying as if alive and dancing to the beat of an inaudible drum.

It's spreading. The damned stuff is spreading in the dark.

That single thought, even more than the sight of the slightly deflated body of the woman who had been a friend, was what sent her, scurrying and suddenly breathless, back to the safety of her well-lit house.

She had to stop on the porch outside the window to compose herself.

The kids will need me calm. They can't see me like this.

All of her instincts were now telling her to run—gather up the kids, as much food as she could, and head for somewhere quiet out of town, somewhere there wouldn't be the dead body of a friend in the yard. She went back into the house determined to start packing, just as the phone beeped at her again.

I forgot the text message.

She called up the message. It was just three words—but they were enough to put paid to any idea of leaving—for the time being at least.

The text was from Shaun.

I'm coming home.

7

It was mid-afternoon in Banff before Shaun pulled out of the Mineral Springs Hospital car park, went up the ramp to the highway and pointed his pickup due east.

Joe had died ten minutes earlier—a minute before Shaun sent the text message to Becky. The infection—that's what the doc called it—killed the big man fast. His hand had been mostly taken before they got out of the mountains—it was a mass of crawling chaos by the time they ditched the plow in the logging company warehouse and switched to Shaun's pickup.

But it was the things that crawled across Joe's scalp that Shaun could not get out of his mind. Worms. That's what it looked most like—brown worms, a nest of them, slowly creeping across Joe's head and across his face. By the time Shaun reached the hospital, got Joe moving in a stumbling, rolling run, and screamed to an orderly for help, the brown fibers were reaching into his eyes and ears. Even then Joe had enough strength left in him to take Shaun's hand and squeeze it hard.

"Don't leave me, pal. Please? Don't leave me—not like those poor souls up at the cabins."

So Shaun had stayed, while the docs tried to stop the spread of the infection. Within half an hour of their arrival, it started to rain outside, and that's when things got really hectic. Shaun stayed close to Joe's side but it was obvious from the ruckus in the corridors and public spaces of the small hospital that something major was going down.

Joe lay there almost covered in brown fiber now, only nostrils and mouth showing through a death mask of matted tissue. Shaun left the dying man long enough to go to the door of the small recovery room and look out.

Medical staff rushed everywhere, voices were raised, people screamed. And overhead, rain kept drumming on the roof. Doctors and nurses led patients through the corridors whose exposed skin was dotted in small, bloody sores and rutted with scratches and weals. Shaun kept thinking about Joe, the red weal on his hand and the itchy scalp he'd worried at for mere minutes before the infection made itself visible.

If it's in the rain, we're in trouble.

And judging by the frantic activity all around the hospital, the trouble was getting worse by the second.

Joe died minutes after that without saying another word—and the docs could do nothing to save him. His nostrils and mouth closed up in a tangled mess of fibrous tissue, his chest heaved, just once, and that was it—all trace of the big man had gone.

Shaun didn't wait for the docs to confirm it. He left the room, took out his phone and tried to reach home—but all he got was a busy signal. He tried a text—and this time had better luck. He thought of all the things he could tell Becky, and of all the things he wanted to say. Then he thought of her there, with the boys, watching the news and seeing that there was trouble out in Banff.

He had sent the message, and now headed for the pickup. The rain shower had stopped by the time he reached the car park, and although the sky was gray and lowering he took the chance, sprinting for the truck and almost throwing himself inside. He thought of heading for the motel to get his luggage, but he had his wallet and phone—anything else wasn't worth wasting the extra time on.

Now he was on the highway, heading east for Calgary.

I'm coming home, baby.

If he'd thought there was chaos in the hospital, it was nothing compared to the scenes at Calgary airport. Shaun had hoped to ditch the pickup and get a flight most, if not all, of the way home to Newfoundland. But the sight of the list of delayed flights on the main concourse and the shouting matches at the check-in counters were more than enough to tell him that nothing was getting out—at least not by air—for a while yet.

He collared the only airport employee who didn't look flustered.

"What's the story?" he asked.

The short woman looked Shaun up and down first, as if sizing up his potential to turn into a screaming banshee, then answered calmly.

"It's countrywide. No flights until further notice. Borders are closed too. Best thing to do is find somewhere safe and sit it out."

"Sit what out?" Shaun asked, afraid that he already knew the answer. The woman waved him toward where a crowd had formed beneath a bank of televisions.

"Don't quote me," she said. "But it looks like everything is going to shit fast. I'm out of here and heading for home as soon as this shift ends—sooner if I get a chance."

That was all she said, but by that time all of Shaun's attention was on the news on the screens. His first thought made him even more determined to get home as quickly as he could manage.

It's not just around here.

As could be expected, the news reports focused on the big cities—the mounds of bodies, the devastated vegetation being much to the fore. Shaun saw London, falling into riots and mayhem that were mirrored in cities all across the planet. He watched the tracking camera shot across the Great Plains that showed the growing circles of brown, and saw the scenes of death in Central Park, New York. It was that scene that got him moving—not towards the check-ins, but back out toward the car park and his pickup, slowing just long enough to buy a carrier bag full of sandwiches, several water bottles and—*Becky, forgive me*—a couple of packs of smokes.

As he pulled out of Calgary and back onto the highway—he had to skirt three different accidents to do so—it was starting to get dark.

The first hour went so easily that he almost relaxed. He kept near—or just over—the speed limit, ignoring the faster traffic that sped past him as if they were on their way to a fire. There was no sign of any accidents here on the main Trans-Canada Highway—a road that would take him most of the way home if he could stay on it—and it was dry, with a clearing sky. He was starting to hope.

Slow and steady does it—it's a long way home.

Now that he was on the open road he had time to think about logistics. Given the chaos he'd seen on the television screens he was unsure how long his credit cards would be accepted as valid tender, but he had a couple of hundred in cash in his wallet that should see him well enough for gas and provisions. Then there was the problem of getting across to The Rock—but he'd deal with that one when he had to.

He'd felt guilty when he'd lit up the first smoke just before leaving Calgary, but after a few he slipped back into the habit as if the last ten years had never happened.

Sorry, Becky. But at least I know I can quit again—if I'm given the time.

He ran the air conditioner rather than wind down a window. Okay, it seemed dry out there, but he knew all too well that weather was a changeable concept at the best of times here in Canada—and it seemed to be far from the best of times.

He watched the gas meter closely—he'd have to stop soon, but he wanted to put a bit more distance away from Calgary before then. He smoked, and tried to find something on the radio that wouldn't make him worry. That was harder than he'd have hoped, for most of the FM stations were running wall-to-wall news, none of it good. More worrying still, some of the stations that he knew should be there were just broadcasting dead air. He selected an old favorite CD instead, and motored east to the pound of ZZ Top for a while until the gas meter was finally low enough that he had to do something about it.

He saw a sign, then lights in the distance a few minutes later. He pulled onto the service station off-ramp—only to find himself at the rear of a line of thirty of more vehicles, sitting still on the forecourt and stretched back to the off-ramp itself, all waiting for a turn at the pumps.

He checked his fuel gauge again—fifty miles left. *Maybe.* It would be a risk, but the line didn't seem to be moving.

But upon looking in his mirror to check it was safe to reverse back off the ramp, he found he had left it too late. Two large trucks had pulled up tight behind him, leaving him no room to back up or even to wiggle his way out.

Seems I'm here for the duration.

He switched off his engine—no sense in wasting more fuel than he had to—lit up a fresh smoke, and tried to find some calm from the worry that threatened to consume him.

The line moved at a snail's pace—one vehicle length every five minutes or so, and Shaun was getting close to screaming in frustration. The radio news told of increasing troubles all across the planet; a storm ran through France, Belgium and Germany and left tens of thousands infected, killing all vegetation in its path. The aftermath brought rioting in the streets of the major cities, and out-of-control fires where the populace tried to burn out the contagion before it spread.

It was all happening too fast for anyone to process, but one talking head's sound bite stayed in Shaun's mind, long after he'd turned the radio off and looked to more ZZ Top for comfort.

This might be the way the world ends.

It took more than two hours to reach the head of the line. Shaun was starting to fret about the tanks being emptied before he even got there—the truck that got to the pump straight ahead of him sucked gas for an age before the driver was satisfied.

Once it was Shaun's turn he did the same, over-filling the tank as much as he dared before heading inside to stand in another line to make his payment. The gas station had a small store; normally it would be full of snacks, coffee, more sandwiches and even some liquor alongside automobile supplies, but there was precious little of anything left on the shelves, and the two girls behind the counter looked frazzled and worn.

"I didn't realize it had got this bad," the guy in front of Shaun said.

"Mister," the girl replied. "This is the worst fucking day of my life—and I don't see it getting any better."

After that Shaun paid, gave the same girl a thin smile that didn't get a reply, and headed at speed back out to his pickup. It was only as he drove out of the forecourt and out from under the huge carport that he noticed it.

Heavy, greasy raindrops spattered against his windscreen, leaving smears behind when he tried to wash them away. He was so intent on the wipers that he took his eyes off the road ahead and was only aware there was a problem when he saw the flare of orange and the sudden flash as someone spun across the road less than a hundred yards ahead. He had no time to even think about braking—he was going too fast. He slowed, swerved as far to the shoulder of the road as he dared, and passed a three-car pile-up with less than a foot to spare, coming to a stop some twenty feet farther up the road. His hand was on the car door before he remembered—it was raining.

Someone dragged their body out of the wreckage of one of the cars behind, and immediately started to claw and scratch at their face, their hands, their arms—a horrible parody of a dance. Behind the accident, farther back along the road, Shaun saw the more headlights approaching, more traffic arriving on the scene.

The screaming, dancing figure was a young lad, no more than twenty. He staggered forward, up to the back of Shaun's pickup and slammed his hands, hard, on the rear window, leaving bloody smears all down the glass. Shaun heard the boy shout—distant, but clear enough.

"Help me. Please, help me."

Once again Shaun's hand went to the door, then pulled back.

I can't go out there. I just can't.

And neither could he stay, for to do so would be to admit that the fear had him paralyzed. He put his foot on the pedal and sped off, accelerating away until the dancing figure was lost in the darkness behind him.

His hands shook badly as he lit up another smoke, and the back wipers smeared blood along with the greasy raindrops, but after a couple of minutes the rain eased again, and the cigarette—illicit pleasure that it was—did much to calm him.

There was now nothing but darkness behind and in front,

only the pickup headlights and the strip of road that kept van-
ishing below him, every meter of it bringing him closer to a
place where he could—maybe—manage to forget the dancing
man.

He muttered his new mantra to himself as he sped into the
black.

I'm coming home, Becky. I'm coming home.

8

The loss of amphibian species across the world from chytrid-iomycosis—an infectious disease caused by the fungal pathogen Batrachochytrium dendrobatidis (Bd)—has been described as "the most spectacular loss of vertebrate biodiversity due to disease in recorded history."

Rohit was surprised to look up at the clock and see it was past midnight. He'd spent the evening in study of the mycelia on the slide under his microscope, and what with that, and monitoring the progress of samples he'd embedded on agar on a row of petri dishes, time had slipped away from him. It wasn't for the first time. He found the sights of the world under his scope endlessly fascinating—a microcosm which, for that particular slide under that particular scope, existed just for him and him alone. It was all too easy to get lost in its wonders, especially when he got a chance to look at something completely new. New, and very worrying.

The samples to his left caused him the most concern. He had hoped to check the infection's growth patterns on different substrates, but there seemed little difference in the mycelia behavior—whatever you fed it on, provided it was carbon based, the fungus flourished. It ate sugars, alcohol, wood—and most alarmingly of all, plastics. Most of Rohit's dishes were glassware, but the petri dish farthest away from him, a rare clear plastic one, was a tangled ruin of brown fibers—fibers that had eaten through agar, through the dish itself, and had now started to spread, over and into the wooden tabletop.

Rohit took the only step he could think of. He poured a cup of molar hydrochloric acid over the whole lot, having to step back quickly as the matted fibers hissed and bubbled. The small lab filled up with a stench so noxious that he was forced to step away further, out into the corridor where he watched from a safe distance as the mycelia succumbed to the acid, leaving only a black bubbling goop behind.

He waited while the recycling fans cleared the air in the lab then went back inside. He now knew what the stuff fed on, and at least he now knew one thing that could kill it—but covering the planet in acid wasn't an option that could reasonably be considered viable. He was about to go back to work in search of another way forward when loud screams echoed up the stairwell behind him.

His first thought, to his shame, was to ignore the noises and keep working—go back into the lab, close the door, and maybe turn up some music. But the screams were getting louder by the second—more frantic, filled with a pain he could only imagine. His better nature took hold, and he headed for the stairs.

As soon as he started on his way down he realized that the clamor from below could only be coming from the cafeteria. He had thought that the place must have been emptied some hours ago; it normally closed for the night at nine, and students had better—or worse—things to be doing. But when he arrived at the foot of the stairs it was to find a small group of some six youths standing over a crawling figure on the ground, obviously the source of what were now continual screams of pain.

He recognized the standing students first—they were the same group who had been sitting by the television, quiet and subdued earlier. And now they seemed even quieter, confused even. Almost as one they turned and stared at Rohit as he came down the last set of stairs, and again he recognized the look.

They're looking to me for guidance. I'm the authority figure here.

He felt anything but authoritative as he walked towards the group, but as soon as he saw who—or rather what—they stood over, his instincts took over. It was a girl, barely into her twenties by the look of things, though it was also something else. A

William Meikle

mass of brown matted mycelia covered much of her lower body, from waist to toes; it looked almost like fur in the dim light.

Rohit saw the woman behind the food counter start to come over, then change her mind. He shouted to her, his voice too loud even above the wails of pain from the girl on the floor.

"Bleach. Fetch me some bleach—and hot towels."

He bent to the girl, who raised a hand toward him. It too was covered in crawling mycelia. One of the lads, a burly youth, bent to take her wrist, but Rohit swatted him away.

"Don't touch any of the mycelia—the brown stuff—just don't touch it. It's infectious, and it spreads fast."

The lad stepped back fast, as if he'd been slapped, but Rohit didn't have time to deal with wounded pride. He had a girl to try to save, although in his heart he knew he was already too late—far too late.

But I have to try, if only for these who are watching. They need me to try.

The woman—he still didn't even know her name—arrived with a bottle of bleach and a hot, damp towel just as he bent toward the prone girl. Her screams had lost a deal of their strength, and were now little more than a thin whine that was somehow worse than the screams—the piteous wail of a beast in pain it didn't know how to handle.

Rohit tried to keep his voice soft and calm.

"Try to keep still. I'm here to help," he said. He poured bleach onto the towel then looked for a spot where he might try to use it. Two brown strands ran, like burst blood vessels, on the girl's cheeks, so he started there. And at first, he seemed to be having some success—the fungus smeared off the cheek and onto the towel where it left only a greasy streak. But even as Rohit stopped rubbing to apply more bleach to the towel, a new line of brown, pencil thin but growing noticeably, started just beneath the girl's left nostril and started crawling across her cheek. And this time, when he rubbed, it didn't remove the strand.

It's under her skin. She's already riddled with the stuff.

"Help her," another of the watching students said, although they didn't move to come to Rohit's side. "For pity's sake, help her."

Rohit kept rubbing bleach on the stricken girl's infection, but he was getting increasingly sure it was all for show—something to let the watchers think that there was a chance of getting rid of the mycelia. Rohit already knew better.

This thing is even more voracious than I feared. We're definitely in serious trouble.

The girl died five minutes later, the fungal fibers filling her throat and nostrils, even running, like brown burst blood vessels, through her eyeballs. Three of the students had a conspiratorial confab at a corner seat, then left quickly. A minute or so later Rohit heard a car rev up outside, and saw a wash of light as the headlights turned away toward downtown St. John's.

"They won't find it's any better there," Rohit murmured, then realized the remaining students had heard him. He motioned one of them forward. "Give me a hand with the body—we need to get her out of here before it spreads further."

"What do you mean, spreads further?" the tall lad he'd spoken to replied. "Is she contagious?"

I think everything's contagious now.

He didn't voice that thought—to give it form would be to acknowledge the truth of it, and Rohit wasn't quite ready to face that just yet.

"Just follow my lead," he said to the youth. "Don't touch any of the infection, and move fast. Are you with me?"

The boy—he looked to be barely out of his teens—looked as if he might throw up, but he bent to Rohit's aid when motioned forward, and helped him half-carry, half-drag the body back out the door and into the parking lot. Rohit waited until they were a good twenty yards from the door before stopping, and let the body drop. It hit the hard surface with a moist thud that also sent up a sudden stench of rot.

"This will have to be far enough," Rohit said, and turned away.

"We can't just leave her here," the boy said "It's not right."

"It'd be even less right to leave her lying on the cafeteria floor, don't you think?" Rohit replied, and leaving the boy standing over the body, went quickly back inside, took the bleach

with him into the kitchen and stood over a sink washing and
rubbing his hands until they were raw and chapped. The boy
joined him before he was done, and after drying, they checked
each other for any signs of brown filaments, even rolling up
their sleeves to check wrists and forearms.

Finally, Rohit pronounced them both clear—for now.

"Check yourself every five minutes," he told the lad. "And
tell me straight away if you notice anything. We will all need to
be extra vigilant from now on."

After washing, he took a bleach-drenched mop out into the
cafeteria and mopped down the spot where the girl had fallen,
then continued across the whole area between there and the
door. The girl's body, which looked somehow deflated and collapsed now, lay out in the car park where they had left her—
dumped her—but Rohit felt no qualms about the deed.

My duty, such as it is, is to the living.

He dragged his gaze away from the dead girl and washed
down the doorframe and the door itself with bleach, twice for
good measure. As he walked back towards the silent group
huddled in the center of the cafeteria, he saw that they were
once again looking to him for a way forward. And there was
something else in their eyes now that hadn't been there before—
it looked like hope.

The woman from the coffee shop—he now saw her name on
a tag on her breast pocket, Irene—hovered around, uncertain of
her role in the situation.

She needs something to do. We all do.

"Would it be possible to get some coffee, please?" Rohit said.
"I think it's going to be a long night."

9

Jim Noble came groggily up out of sleep. He was in his bunk on the boat, and he only just remembered getting there, sometime around nine, when the day had finally caught up with him and Kerry had insisted—ordered—that he take some downtime. He'd fallen on top of the sheets, fully clothed and still in his hazmat suit and fell asleep in seconds, despite his mind racing with images of spreading filaments, gunfire and flames—and the smell, the God-awful smell, of rot and burning flesh.

He could still taste it now, and felt a gag reflex in his throat that forced him out of the bunk making for the small head at the back of the cabins. His headgear—hood and mask—slid to the ground at his feet, fallen from where he'd left it at the foot of the bunk, and he didn't have the energy to bend to retrieve it. It was all he could manage to strip off the gloves. He rolled up his sleeves while standing over the small washbasin—and there it was.

What had been a red scrape on his wrist was now traced through with fine brown filaments. It was no more than the size of a thumbnail, but the edges were already spreading out into the skin beyond the red mark.

I'm infected.

He scraped at the filaments with the forefinger of his other hand. The brown material slid across his skin in a single piece, leaving a weeping sore behind. He wrapped the scab up in a piece of tissue paper and flushed it away.

Maybe I caught it in time?

He held the flesh wound up to the light. There was still the taint of brown there, faint but definitely present. He rubbed harder, then harder still until blood flowed—deep red, thank-fully—if it had been brown and watery he might have ended himself right there and then. Washing the wound out with soap made it sting and throb, but it finally looked clean—or as clean as he was going to get it. He smothered the area with disinfectant cream from a tube in the small cupboard above the basin, then bandaged it up, tight, as if hiding it away might make it disap-pear from his mind. Rolling down the sleeve of the hazmat suit hid it away further, and the wound had even stopped throb-bing—for now at least.

I caught it in time. I'll be fine.

He was about to head for his bunk again when Kerry came to the door.

"George Street is on fire."

"One of the bars?"

"No—all of it."

For a while, Jim was too busy to worry about his bandaged wrist.

10

Rebecca sat on the armchair—*Shaun's chair*—staring at the news unfolding on the television, her mind only half on it, the other half full of what she'd seen out in the garden.

Patty's gone.

When she'd got back inside, she'd checked on the girl, who seemed soundly asleep on the sofa, almost hidden under the throw apart from the very top of her head. Then she'd gone up and stood at the boys' door for long seconds before going in—afraid that she might find them, buried in a crawling mat of brown worms. But both of the boys were sound asleep, Mark, as usual, hanging half out of bed with an arm dragging on the floor, and Adam rolled up in a curled bag made of his bedclothes.

She had gone downstairs and poured herself a stiff glass of rye, and she drank it in one swallow, barely noticing the liquor on its way down. Then she sat in the chair that always felt several sizes too big for her, and now she was still there, several hours later, still trying to process the events of the previous day, as well as those that were unfolding on the news on the big screen.

Things had got a lot worse just in the past few hours. Daylight came in the Far East over cities in turmoil and countries with crops, forests and grasslands all riddled with brown circles of infection. North Korea decided it was South Korea's fault—or maybe Japan's—and launched a series of missile attacks. Japan retaliated, Russia got pissed off, and now the whole region was fighting both the infection and each other.

Things weren't much better farther west. Israel closed down its borders and went into lockdown; Iran and Iraq accused each

other of biological warfare; Russia and Ukraine were at each other's throats again, and might be fighting if Russia wasn't quite
so busy with the Korean situation, and Pakistan was threatening to nuke India. The worst of the rioting was affecting the
capital cities of Europe. Paris burned, Rome was a seething fight
between police and mob, and the center of London had been
completely abandoned to the looters as the authorities were
stretched far beyond the limits of their capabilities for control.

And all the time, while the squabbling went on, it was still
raining, somewhere, sending more of the infection down to the
ground to fester and spread—and kill. Rebecca turned to the
local news channel in search of some relief, but there was little
forthcoming. A curfew had been declared across The Rock for
the rest of the night. Anyone caught outside in St. John's was
going to be arrested and taken to a temporary refuge set up
in Hamilton Park High School Hall—there were already several hundred people there. Although the camera shot cut away
quickly, it wasn't fast enough to avoid showing that many of
those present showed signs of the same infection that had got
Patty Payne.

There was a major fire in the downtown area. The television
crews weren't being allowed close enough to show pictures, but
the red in the night sky all along George Street—and up the hill
beyond—told Rebecca that the fire was a big one. The old town
was never going to be the same again.

Residents were being asked to stay in their homes, and lock
all doors and windows— no one in, no one out seemed to be the
rule, and an Army unit from the barracks was out in protective
clothing in the streets trying to enforce it. If she hadn't known
any better, Rebecca might think she was watching a movie
rather than a news report from so close to home.

The reality of what was going on was starting to hit her.
This wasn't a small inconvenience. She wouldn't be talking
about it with the other parents in the schoolyard in the morning, wouldn't be chatting over the till at the shops. In fact, it
might be a while before she got near a shop again.

That thought got her moving. She spent an hour taking
inventory. Luckily the pantry and fridge were well stocked, and

she had plenty of water in bottles in the garage, as well as a chest freezer full of meat, fish and frozen vegetables.

A couple of weeks' worth—if the power holds—then a couple of days after that on the generator.

Being prepared was Shaun's thing—a Newfoundland winter is always unpredictable, and power outages were a common occurrence. That preparedness was going to stand Rebecca in good stead—for a time at least.

But any feeling of well-being disappeared completely when she returned to the living area. The throw had been discarded in a heap at the side of the sofa, and the sliding door out to the porch lay wide open. There was no sign of the girl, but Rebecca could take a good guess at where she might have gone.

This time, before venturing outside, she went down to the garage and fetched Shaun's big flashlight, checking that it was working before going back to the main room. Even then, she stood just inside the door for long seconds, trying to muster up the courage to step outside. It was the thought of the young girl in peril that finally got her moving.

Patty would never forgive me if I left her baby out there in the dark.

She switched on the flashlight and swept the beam over the yard. Fresh footsteps in grass damp with dew showed her that Annie had indeed headed for where her mother had fallen, but the beam wasn't strong enough to reach that far back in the yard, beyond showing Rebecca clumps of shadows, darker against the background.

She stepped off the porch.

"Annie? Come back inside sweetheart. You'll catch your death out here."

She got no reply. She stepped off the porch and started following the tracks in the grass, headed for the dark end of the yard where she'd left Patty's body.

She found Annie right where she expected the girl to be, lying on top of her dead mother, both locked in embrace. Rebecca bent and with her free hand reached for Annie's wrist, but when she tugged, both bodies came with her. And Annie didn't register her presence at all. Rebecca shone the flashlight

full on the girl's face, only to see a brown, dry, death mask of
fibers. Annie had come out to meet her mother, had found what
she was looking for, and had joined her in her fate. Not only
that, it looked like the joining had become more than figura-
tive—where the girl's bare arm touched Patty's body the arm
and the body had become one mass of matted flesh and fiber.
At the rate the bodies were being consumed, it would not be
long before they looked like the pelicans in London—they were
quickly being reduced to mere mounds of brown wormy tissue.

There was something else too. The grass for a foot and more
in a circle around the bodies was brown, and the earth below
seemed to seethe and roil. Rebecca stepped back fast as she
noticed her shoes had just infringed on the browned area.

She took one last look at the two bodies, allowed herself a
sob and a single tear, then wiped her eyes and went back to the
house in search of the kerosene.

The bodies burned fast, going up in a whoosh like so much
dry kindling. Within a matter of a minute or so there was nothing there to signify that Patty and her daughter had ever been.
Rebecca also dumped the throw from the sofa on the flames—
there was no sign of any infection on it, but she wasn't prepared
to take any chances, not with the two boys to look after. The
flames spread in a circle, burning across the whole spread of the
browned area. The flames had a peculiar blue-tinged quality
that reminded Rebecca of propane burning more than of anything else.

As she finally turned away she saw that the skyline to the
northeast, over the downtown area of the city, was tinged in
reds and yellows. They were still having fires of their own over
there—and she wasn't sure that she wanted to know how much
was burning.

She went back inside, closed the porch door firmly, and sat
in the big chair, drinking more rye and staring, unseeing, at the
television while tears ran, untended, down her cheeks.

11

Shaun tried to keep his driving smooth, cruising at or near the speed limit. He still had a long haul ahead of him. He figured on probably three days' driving—and that was just to get to Montreal. And given the reports of shootings and rioting he was hearing, it might be best to keep as far away from larger population centers as he could, for a while at least.

He was starting to regret leaving Calgary. Although there were no reports of any flights being allowed up, the Canadian government spokesman on the most recent news broadcast had suggested that the situation was well in hand and that normal service would resume shortly. Then again, it was a government man talking, and Shaun trusted them as much as he did a wet fart. He'd aim for Montreal—and if the news improved, he might be able to ditch the pickup at the airport there and fly straight home. He certainly hoped so, for Becky and the boys were getting bigger in his mind all the time and the worry ate hard at him.

He hadn't seen any more accidents since that last big one—hadn't seen much of any traffic at all—there was just him, his smokes, and what he could make out in the headlights. If it wasn't for the news on the radio he might even enjoy the drive. He'd tried more ZZ Top, and then some rock FM channels, but the need to know grew bigger than the need not to so he kept the news on. It meant he smoked more to compensate, but he'd stopped feeling guilty about that vice hours ago.

As he drove on into the night, the news reports grew increasingly frantic. He didn't have the benefit of pictures, but the reporters did more than enough to help him imagine the scenes of mayhem and carnage in the cities, and the slow, almost silent, destruction of the green places of the world. He remembered the forest clearing, and the deathly quiet they'd found there.

Is that what's waiting for us all?

At least some details of what was happening were now coming out. The general consensus was that it was fungal. The cause of its sudden appearance was somewhat more obscure, but that didn't stop the talking heads from speculating, from GMO gone bad, to global warming to *fucking aliens* and all points in between. What was indisputable was that it was happening on a grand scale, a planetwide phenomenon that was bringing war and confusion along with it. The veneer of civilization hadn't taken long to be stripped away, especially in the hot spots where it had been thin to start with. The worrying thing was that the commentators had started to speculate which would be the first country to throw a nuke into the mix—and they weren't talking about if, they were talking about when.

What nobody seemed to be talking about was how to stop the spread of the infection. Cross border cooperation on a grand scale was going to be needed, and nobody as yet had stepped up to the plate to start organizing any such campaign, with each country being too busy firefighting in its own jurisdiction.

It was while he was listening to that particular sound bite that he noticed he had started to drift across the road, and had to swerve to compensate, glad that there was no one in the outside lane. Tiredness was starting to seep in.

And I'm no use to Becky and the kids if I get smeared all over the highway.

He turned the air conditioning to cool—normally he'd open a window, but he was tired, not stupid. He was good for maybe another hour—he knew that from experience—so he started looking for somewhere he could pull off and rest up, and fill the tank again.

He saw the lights in the distance half an hour later and pulled off at the slip road when he saw the sign that proclaimed it to be the last services for the next hundred kilometers.

The forecourt was brightly lit, almost dazzling after the

relative darkness out on the highway. All the pumps were free; he was the only customer, but that in itself wasn't unusual for this hour of the night.

He checked overhead, and out on the concrete he could see under the lights, before stepping out of the car—all seemed dry, and he filled up the tank with one eye on the carport canopy above. It looked solid enough, but if it started raining he didn't want to be under any drips.

The tank sucked another eighty bucks' worth. If it kept draining his wallet at this rate he was going to be pushed to make it anywhere near home with the cash at hand. He considered just getting back in the pickup and driving off, but the last thing he needed was a cop on his tail, even if he thought the chances were slim that there would be anyone willing to chase him, on this of all nights. He locked up the pickup—better safe than sorry tonight—and went inside the station to pay up.

He quickly wished he'd given in to his first instinct.

Like the scene at his first stop, the shelves of the small station store had been emptied of everything of worth. But where things had seemed to have happened in an orderly fashion earlier, this place had clearly been looted, and with some force, for there was blood spatter on the liquor cabinet, and a smeared trail on the floor near the till. It was the trail that caught his attention. It was obviously blood, or had been, for it was now equally obviously something else—brown threads ran through it, and even from a distance he saw that they were most definitely still alive, sinuously weaving their way through the red.

He followed the trail around the counter, and found the youngster that had been in charge of the station for the night. The shotgun wounds in his chest had probably killed him, but the brown threads were quickly making sure there wasn't anything left worth burying.

The till lay open—and empty, the money too having been looted. Shaun was already starting to wonder whether even his cash was going to be of much use any more. There was certainly no one here who was in any state to accept payment for the gas.

He backed out of the store, vigilant against the slightest sound or movement, but there was only the faintest flicker of neon, the soft hissing of the tubes being the sole sound in the too-quiet night.

He was paying so much attention to what might come at him from inside the store that he didn't spot the man at his back until it was almost too late. He heard a voice first.

"I'm going to need the keys for that truck of yours, mister."

The words sounded slurred, as if the speaker might be drunk; but on turning round to face the man, Shaun saw immediately the cause of the speech impediment. It was a tall rangy man in denims and cowboy boots. That was below the waist—where he still looked like a man. Above that his clothes were awash with drying blood—and more of the brown threads of infection. Threads crawled over his chest, up the left side of his neck, and over that whole half of his face, creeping into the corner of his mouth, up his left nostril, and thankfully covering the eye on that side, although the socket already looked sunken, somewhat hollow. Shaun saw all that almost before he spotted the shotgun that was now aimed at his chest.

"I said, I'm going to need your truck, mister," the man said. One of the hands on the gun was also covered in the brown filaments. Fine threads ran over fingers, thumb and wrist to where it then grew, not up the man's sleeve, but over it, meshing and matting into what had once been a leather jacket but was just more of the brownish tissue. The man looked barely able to stand—indeed the barrel of the shotgun had already headed south, now pointing at somewhere around Shaun's knees.

"Are you deaf, fucker?" the man said, and tried to lift the weapon, but the weight of it had become too much for him. Shaun took his chance and stepped forward, kicking out and knocking the stock out of the man's hand—dismayingly, it took a chunk of meat with it, leaving the attacker staring dumbly at a hand that was now just a thumb and forefinger. There was no blood, just more of the brown tissue.

Shaun stepped back quickly as the man threw a punch. The act of doing so sent the tall cowboy off balance, teetering into the wall of the service station to fall in a heap on the concrete. He showed no sign of trying to get up. He held the ravaged hand up in front of his good eye, and studied it as dispassionately as if it were a piece of steak. He seemed to have forgotten Shaun completely.

The shotgun lay some three feet away. Shaun considered taking it, but it still had bits of flesh adhered to the stock, and Shaun hadn't suddenly gone stupid. He kicked the weapon away sending it skittering across the concrete to vanish into the darkness beyond the limits of the carport. The prone man didn't make any effort to complain. He still wasn't showing any signs of wanting to get up either, and Shaun was in no mood to give him any help.

He turned away, heading for the pickup. That did get the cowboy's attention.

"You'll see it for yourself soon enough," he called out as Shaun kept walking away. "You'll see the blue hills and the things that live there. And then you'll know."

Shaun kept walking and didn't look back.

Two minutes later, as he drove the pickup out of the service station, he saw that the cowboy had started to crawl across the concrete, heading for the darkness, pulling himself along with his arms—and leaving a trail of brown and red slime behind him as he went.

12

Somehow Rohit had become the man in charge of the small group who spent the night around the television in the cafeteria. Three students, and the coffee shop assistant, Irene, all looked to him whenever any kind of decision needed to be made— whether it was about the safety of using the washrooms, the need for more coffee, or the undesirability of venturing beyond the doors of the building. There was also the fact that just watching the news brought far more questions than answers. Rohit explained what he knew about how fungal infections spread, about how it might be contained, and how much trouble he thought they were in. But it seemed to go in one ear and out the other for the listeners, as if their fear had stripped all of their faculties for retaining the information.

More than anything, Rohit wanted to head upstairs to his lab, disinfect the area, and lock himself in with enough food to last for a while. But the group around the television—the students in particular—seemed a lot younger than they had before the situation went to hell, as if the terror and chaos had laid bare their true selves.

I cannot abandon them.

His original plan had been to just see out the night—drink coffee, watch news and wait for the cavalry to arrive and save the day. But from what they saw on the television, it was apparent that the authorities had more than enough on their plates without worrying about people who were hiding in relative safety.

And then there was the elephant in the room; or rather, the body in the car park. Rohit saw the students—all of them at one point or another over the course of the night—look in that direction, then just as quickly look away. No one spoke of the dead girl, no one mentioned what had happened, and if anyone was bothered by the stinging smell of bleach that hung around the cafeteria, nobody mentioned it. Instead, the television became the main focus of attention as it reeled off catastrophe after catastrophe, crisis after crisis, until Rohit felt quite numb and incapable of further surprise, as if he'd watched too many big dumb action movies in too short a time period.

One of the students—Steve, he was starting to get the names straight now—banged his phone on the table, hard enough to crack the case.

"Piece of shitty, shit shit," he shouted, threw the phone away across the floor, and buried his face in his hands, weeping. Nobody moved to comfort him. It wasn't the first outburst of the night; it was almost as if they'd been taking turns. Rohit felt like joining in every time it happened, but his composure held—so far.

Besides, we're well off compared to some of those poor souls on the news.

The worldwide death toll was already estimated to be well into the tens of millions, and rising every second. Los Angeles was in flames, as was Berlin, Paris and large parts of London. There was a war on in the Far East, but details were sketchy and chaotic at best. And the next nuke had been deployed— China again, and a city of two million people downwind from the original site, a city that was now just a pile of ash and ruin.

Somewhere, it rained.

He had checked his hands for infection every five minutes since moving the body outside, half-expecting at any moment to see the first faint trace of brown that would tell him that death was coming. But he was clean—so far.

He had the rest of the group check themselves at intervals— everybody was still clear—they'd been lucky, and contained it before it could spread. But Rohit was all too aware of the insidious nature of this threat. Fungi got everywhere. Most people rarely noticed it until it became a problem, but it was there—in timbers and joists, in flooring, lurking just under the surface in lawns and gardens, inside walls and climbing up trees. It did what it did—and it did it very well.

And now, it seems it has learned to do it even better.

He was brought out of a reverie by a shout from another of the students.

"Doctor Patel, there's something weird on the television."

That's a bit of an understatement.

But the girl was right. This latest report was stranger still than anything that had gone before. The reporter looked grave and solemn as he read from what was obviously a prepared message.

"The public is being asked to report any knowledge they may glean about the Blue Hills. I repeat, please use the number at the bottom of your screens to report any knowledge or information pertinent to the Blue Hills."

A 555-number rolled across the bottom of the picture—Rohit committed it to memory, just in case, but he couldn't figure out the meaning of the request, although something stirred at the back of his mind.

"So what are the Blue Hills?" the girl—Anna, he remembered—asked, looking straight at Rohit, who could only shrug.

"I can't say yet. But it rings a bell. I need to go up to my lab. Sit tight and don't do anything stupid. I won't be more than ten minutes."

Nobody wanted to go with him, the rest being more than happy to stay in the light and warmth around the television set. That suited Rohit just fine—his solitary nature meant that he'd already used up his quota of being around people for the month, if not the year, and he needed some quiet time alone to think, possibly even to plan.

Just the act of climbing up through the quiet—almost too quiet—stairwell did much to re-establish his distance from events both in the cafeteria and in the wider world outside. And five minutes on his laptop—the Wi-Fi to the outside world was still alive—reminded him of the connection his mind had been trying to make for several minutes.

He'd heard of the Blue Hills in a book—he'd picked it up

because it had some giant mushrooms looking over dwarfed human figures on the cover—a potboiler, Edwardian adventure that he'd found rather silly but surprisingly entertaining. He still had the book on his shelf and took it out, flicking through looking for the appropriate paragraph.

Finally he found it.

"I should start by telling you something you don't want to hear," Carnacki said, lighting a cheroot. *"Your bosses will never print what I'm about to tell you. Indeed, you may never even write it up, for I am pretty dashed sure that you will not believe me. Nevertheless, it is all true, if a tad strange to unenlightened ears.*

"I am a student of the arcane," he began. *"A searcher after secrets lost over time in ancient books and scrolls. My studies have, over the years, brought me into direct contact with what I believe the layman would call ghosts and ghoulies, denizens of the Outer Darkness that surrounds us."*

I put up a hand to stop him.

"You've lost me already," I said. *"And I should tell you that I don't believe in any of that hocus-pocus."*

He smiled at me.

"I am long used to that response," he said. *"But hear me out. In the end, it may or may not make sense to you, but at least you will understand why I was in the greenhouse tonight, and what I was doing there.*

"The story begins this morning. I was in my library, testing out a new dynamo and ensuring that the valves on the Electric Pentacle were still functional, when I became aware of a fluctuation in the field. I immediately set up a circle on the floor and sat inside. I called up a spell I have memorized from the Sigsand mss, and the fluctuation resolved itself into a high mesmeric singing that was most pleasant but at the same time rather disconcerting, for there was no apparent source of the sound.

"You may also be pleased to know that I had but ten minutes previously read your article on the opening of the greenhouse. I put two and two together, and immediately set on a course of research into these

singing Mongolian mushrooms of which you seemed so enamored.

"It took me several hours, but the more I uncovered, the less I liked what I had found. There are several legends from widespread places around the world that deal with these fungi, and none of them have much, if anything, good to say about them. The details vary considerably, but on one thing there is perfect agreement. On no account should they be cultivated, or allowed to sporulate, for they are voracious in their appetite, and devious in their methods. Now this would be jolly bad news even if that were all that was involved. But the old texts told more, of a spiritual dimension to the fungi, and of even older tales of their origin millennia ago on the high plains of Leng in the shade of the Blue Hills. Now all of this will sound arcane, if not ridiculous, to your modern sensibilities, Malone. But trust me, I learned enough this afternoon to put me in an awful funk. I came to realize that the singing you found so melodious was merely a precursor to the main event. The fungi were preparing to spore, and if they were allowed to do so an apocalypse of biblical proportions would quickly engulf this city, this country, perhaps even the whole planet."

So there it was, the piece of information he'd been looking for. Rohit knew it was of little to no use, for he could hardly call up the authorities and tell them that he'd found the answer in a science fiction story. Besides, he had found *an* answer, and it could very well be just a coincidence. But there was something about the description he'd read—about the voracious nature of the fungus, and the mention of the Blue Hills—that made him think that the writer of the book may have stumbled, however unwittingly, on a truth that was only now making itself known.

And if it is a truth, it is one I can see no immediate benefit in knowing.

13

Jim Noble was awake—awake, but dreaming.

They'd lost the downtown area in the early hours of the morning. Most of George Street and the southern half of Water Street were still burning, and there wasn't going to be much left of either when the flames subsided. That might even be for the best, given the spread of the infection that they had seen—some of the older wooden buildings were riddled, brown filaments crawling through floor, carpets, walls and roofs.

As dawn rose across the smoke-filled harbor it was to show that the slopes of Shea Heights to the southeast were also infested—brown already crawling high up through the green. The powers that be had, at some point during the night, stopped talking about containment and quarantine. Now it was all about survival—and from what Jim had seen, there weren't going to be that many people left to save.

He should be worried—terrified even—but he felt strangely calm, almost serene. And every time too much worry or doubt tried to creep in, he felt a surge of warmth and well-being and heard a tune, almost a song, in his head. It was a drone, like a chant, that promised peace and contentment, joy and happiness. He was just growing like it, and had spent much of the predawn time in a fugue state, halfway between two worlds. When he closed his eyes he could almost see the other side— Blue Hills and brown land, and a crop that needed tending. It called for him, that far-off place.

But he wasn't ready to go.

Not yet.

He had an itch in his arm he was afraid to scratch, and still harbored fear in his heart for the fate of the town—his town. Duty kept him upright and moving.

But the call was getting stronger.

He was standing on the deck of the boat when Kerry came to his side and handed him a coffee. He slipped off his mask, and saw the look that Kerry tried, unsuccessfully, to hide.

"Christ, Jim, you look like battered shit. Get yourself off to bed for a couple of hours. I'll call if we need you."

Jim shook his head. If he went to bed, the Blue Hills would get him—he didn't know how he knew that, he just knew. He changed the subject, none too subtly.

"The town's lost, isn't it?"

"Not just the town," Kerry said. "Going by the news, it's the whole bloody country—maybe even the planet."

"So what do we do now?"

"They're talking limited evacuation—heading farther north, where it's cold. They don't think this stuff likes the cold. We've been told to start looking for survivors that'll come—and leave the infected, and those that won't leave their homes, to their fates."

Jim was about to protest, then got a hit of calm and the faintest ringing of the chant in his head. All doubt and worry washed away again, leaving him only with the faintest sense of having forgotten something important. Kerry looked at him again, staring into his face,

"You sure you're okay?"

Jim nodded, and swallowed half the coffee, feeling it go straight to his head and set it ringing.

"A couple more of these and I'm ready for round two."

Kerry nodded in reply, and waved a hand to encompass the burning streets of their town.

"This lot's gone. We're ordered up to Stavanger Drive then over to Memorial—they think there might be pockets of survivors in the box stores and at the university, and they want us to make one last check. You ready to roll?"

The song grew in Jim's head again, like a distant choir, calling him home.

He swallowed the last of the coffee and the singing faded away, but not quite completely. He still heard it, voices in the wind, as he went with Kerry down the gangway to the truck.

14

Rebecca was still sitting in the armchair when thin sunlight filtered into the room and the clump of footsteps overheard signaled that the boys were up and moving around.

Her instincts kicked in and for a while she was all *mum*, getting breakfast ready for her and the lads. Mark arrived downstairs first, and was heading for the living area and the television when she called him away, through into the kitchen.

I don't want them seeing what's going on—not yet. I want to tell them myself.

Pancakes and maple syrup mollified any feelings the lad might have of being hard done by, and Rebecca made sure there was plenty of food coming to keep all of them busy for a time once Adam, slower and more sleepy, arrived at the table.

"What's wrong, mum?" the younger boy asked as soon as he sat down. He always had been the more observant of the two, more tuned in to Rebecca's moods.

"I'll tell you later—just eat your breakfast, then you can go play your game while I clear up."

Mark's face lit up in a broad smile.

"No school?"

Rebecca nodded. "No school today. And maybe no school for a while."

Mark's smile got broader still. Adam looked like he had more questions, but she stopped that simply enough by giving him another pancake.

Once they'd finished breakfast, Adam stayed in the kitchen to help with the clearing up while Mark went through to the living area. Rebecca's heart took a leap when he called out seconds later.

"Hey, Ma—there's some kind of brown shit all over the sofa."

She didn't even pause long enough to berate him for bad language; twenty seconds later she had both boys back in the kitchen. They stared at her, wide eyed, as if she'd gone mad as she went to the cupboard under the sink, throwing out cleaning fluid bottles across the floor until she found what she wanted— rubber gloves and a bottle of bleach.

"Stay here," she said. "Right here. Don't move."

Adam started to cry, and Rebecca thought she might join him soon if she didn't get moving herself. She pulled on the rubber gloves, left the boys in the kitchen and, holding the bleach bottle in front of her like a weapon, went through into the main living area.

Mark was right—there was a load of *brown shit* all over the sofa, a mass of matted brown fibers, woven into and through the fabric and clustered at the far end, where Annie had been lying. The first thing Rebecca did was to check that it hadn't spread beyond the structure of the couch. Then she poured half the bleach onto the end that wasn't affected. She opened the patio doors and tried to manhandle the whole thing out into the yard, trying to keep her grip where she'd just applied the bleach. It was too heavy for her, but Mark had been watching from the kitchen door and came over to help.

"Don't get near the brown shit," she said, before she realized who she was talking to. The boy, to his credit, didn't collapse in a fit of giggles; he put his hands near hers on the sofa arm and pushed, hard. In one smooth movement the couch went out the door, across the porch, and fell into the yard. Between the two of them they got it upended, and heaved it away from the house as far as they could manage.

Rebecca stood there, panting.

"You want to tell me why we threw the couch out into the yard, Ma?" Mark said, deadpan.

She wanted to gather him to her in a hug, but there was something else she needed to do first. She went back inside, got a cloth from the kitchen, and mopped down the hardwood floor in the front room with yet more bleach—they'd made some new gouges in it while moving the sofa, but she wasn't about to spend any time fretting about that.

It was only when she was satisfied and stood, panting again, that she realized that the two boys were standing at the sliding door, staring out into the yard. There was something about the way they held themselves—still and stiff—that told Rebecca her boys were terrified.

She went to join them, and felt a shiver of fear of her own.

She hadn't taken the time to look when they threw out the sofa, but now she saw it, all too clearly.

The whole backyard—every bit of wood, plant and greenery—was a dead thing, brown and matted and fibrous, and squirming as if infested with thin worms. The brown area reached all the way up to their porch, and under it.

Rebecca stepped forward as far as she dared to check. The brown worms had already started to spread up the supporting legs of the porch and it wouldn't be long until they started to creep through the boards immediately underfoot.

It's probably already well established under the house.

Ten minutes later she was getting the kids into the SUV, having loaded the trunk with as much food, water and sensible clothing as she could spare the time to throw together. She cast a longing look at the chest freezer—there was so much food there, so much that would be wasted—but she couldn't take it, didn't have any more time for preparations, her mind full of the thought of the brown tendrils, creeping ever closer.

And she had the boys to consider. She'd scared them, badly, with her shrieking insistence that they hurry, and now they were in the back of the SUV, wide-eyed, almost teary.

It'll be okay once we're out on the road.

She said goodbye to the house—she already knew that even if they did come back, it would never be the same again—got in the SUV and, only then, engaged the garage door.

She was glad she waited. The small front lawn was dead and brown, and even the strip of wispy grass that ran between the wheel ruts of the driveway was matted with writhing filaments.

She accelerated out of the garage, almost spinning as she took the turn into the road too sharpish, then sped off down the crescent toward the Ring Road junction.

She didn't look back.

Just being in the back of the SUV and on the move seemed to
have settled the boys. By the time Rebecca turned onto the main
highway they were even bickering about whose turn it was to
get the bigger of the two tablets they had for games-playing.
Rebecca finally started to pay attention to the road and the
world beyond the limits of the SUV.

She quickly came to wish she didn't have to. Vehicles lay,
either abandoned or crashed, along the side of the highway,
both on the hard shoulder and in the ditch beyond that. There
were cars, pickups and trucks—some of them with bodies all
too obviously still slumped in the seats. The verge was the now
familiar dead brown, matted with filaments. Far off to her left,
down in the town, tall palls of smoke rose and drifted out over
the harbor.

The further she got along the highway, the more discarded
or crashed vehicles littered the road, and she had to swerve
wildly on more than one occasion to avoid adding the SUV to
the debris.

Nothing moved on the road but them.

Then, in the distance, she saw that the traffic seemed to
be backed up in a tailback. She slowed until she saw the first
dead body on the road ahead, then two more, on the verge, as if
they'd tried to crawl away. She slowed to almost a walking pace,
creeping past the line of trucks until, at the Irving Station right
at the edge of town, she came to the roadblock—or rather, what
had been a roadblock.

Three army trucks sat partially across the road. It was obvious they had blocked both directions into and out of town at
some point the previous night, and equally obvious that the
blockade had been broken, with some violence, by people intent
on leaving.

Dead bodies lay strewn everywhere she looked. She checked
in the rear-view mirror; luckily the boys were blind to the scenes
outside, lost, heads down, in their games. For once Rebecca was
thankful for their oblivion.

As she drove through the remnants of the blockade she saw something else. It had rained here, sometime in the past hour or so. The road was wet, and so were the bodies, several of which looked bloated to the point of bursting. She saw the cause of the bloating just before she put her foot down hard on the accelerator and pointed the SUV out into open country. A dead man lay, face up, staring sightlessly at the sky—but it was the thing on his chest that drew her gaze—a puffball the size of a pumpkin, bigger even, dusty brown and crenellated. As Rebecca watched it seemed to swell and deflate, twice, as if it was breathing then it exhaled, hard, in an explosion that sent a myriad of tiny spores bursting into the air, spores that rattled and danced on the hood for the SUV even as Rebecca sped away.

She waited until she reached a quiet stretch, and slowed, getting out her phone one-handed. She still couldn't get a signal through to Shaun—but a reply to his text seemed to go somewhere.

She could only hope it reached him.

15

Epigeous sporocarps that are visible to the naked eye, especially fruiting bodies of a more or less agaricoid morphology, are often referred to as mushrooms or, in the case of the genera Calvatia, Calbovista and Lycoperdon, puffballs. In amateur mushroom hunting, and to a large degree in academic mycology as well, identification of higher fungi is based on the features of these sporocarps. Puffball fungi are so called because of the clouds of brown, dust-like spores that are emitted when the mature fruiting body bursts, often in response to impacts such as those of falling raindrops or touch by a passing animal.

The largest known fruiting body is a specimen of Phellinus ellipsoideus (formerly Fomitiporia ellipsoidea) found on Hainan Island. It measures up to 1,085 centimeters in length and is estimated to weigh between 400 and 500 kilograms.

Shaun woke with a start. The last thing he remembered was pulling off to the side of the road, too tired to go any further. He saw by the clock on the dash that he'd slept nearly four hours since then, and the first light of dawn was just showing in the east ahead of him. He was somewhere—hopefully not too far—west of Winnipeg, having driven for hours with his foot to the floor after leaving the service station, his mind full of the sight of the crawling man and the slime trail he was leaving as he moved.

His first action on waking was to reach instinctively for a smoke.

Well, that didn't take long.

It was as he lit up that he noticed something else; there

was a distant drone, barely audible inside the pickup, and definitely coming from out beyond the edge of the road. Before he was aware of it, he'd rolled the window down to hear it better. Immediately it was as if pictures formed in his mind, not dreamlike, but with perfect clarity. He could still see the road in front of the pickup, the sun just rising far on the horizon. But he could also see these new images, of a high plain beneath Blue Hills. Mushrooms grew there, tall oval puffballs, brown and heavily ridged, bent against a stiff wind. But what drew his gaze wasn't the fungi; it was the things that moved among them in that high forest under the purple sky, the slumping, disfigured things that crawled slowly among the stalks, picking delicately at the puffballs with long white tentacles. Even as he watched, one turned in his direction. A face that was little more than a gaping maw topped by a lidless eye that stared at him, through him, down to the depths of his soul.

As the drone increased in volume, Shaun was reminded of nothing less than the sound of a massed band of bagpipers, just about to launch into a tune. He felt drawn to it, compelled even, and his hand went to the door of the truck, intending to open it and step out.

He might even have done so, had his phone not chosen that moment to beep, twice, signifying an incoming text.

Becky!

The vision—if that is what is was—cut off immediately and the drone, although still present, lost much of its enticing allure, enough so that Shaun was able to wind up the window and cut out the noise further. When he switched on the pickup's engine, he couldn't hear any noise from outside, although there was, just at the range of hearing, a sense that someone—something—was calling his name.

He found it easy to ignore as he checked the phone. It was only three words.

Going to mum's.

That told him more than he needed to know—Becky and the kids had left St. John's, on a school day, left the security of the house and town, to head up the coast to a remote community that Becky had always done her best to leave.

Things are worse than I thought.

He sat and smoked the cigarette, waiting to see if any more messages were going to come through, not wanting to miss one while driving. As he sat there he remembered that the stricken man at the service station had spoken to him—and now the words made more sense.

"You'll see the blue hills and the things that live there. And then you'll know."

There were no more texts by the time he finished the smoke. He was about to set off along the road again when he caught a glimpse of movement off to his right. A huge bull moose clambered up onto the highway and started across. Then another, followed by a harem of females and a small herd of young. The beasts kept coming—a flow of wildlife as if a migration was in progress—and not just moose. Shaun watched as elk, white tailed deer, foxes, raccoons, rabbits, several black bears, and even an imperious cougar all headed south to north across the highway in front of him. They all crossed over and went down onto the grasslands beyond the verge.

Only, now that the sun was almost up, he was able to see that there wasn't any grassland anymore. It was a sea of matted brown, from the highway all the way into the far, misty distance. The infected area was punctuated by tall, almost egg-like puffballs and as the horde of beasts walked among then, they puffed, sending out choking clouds of dust-like spores. The beasts fell—none of them struggled—and immediately began to become assimilated.

Shaun knew exactly what was happening.

Feeding time.

And as the animals finally stopped coming, and he was able to drive away, he realized that the drone had called them, had taken them—and that his car engine was the only thing stopping him from succumbing in the same manner.

He put the ZZ Top disc back on and turned up the volume as he headed east, in search of somewhere—anywhere—that might be safe.

His mind felt like a jigsaw puzzle with too many missing pieces—Becky was right there, front and center as always, and his worry for her and the boys was huge and almost too much to bear. But there was also the crawling man in the gas station, the animals, meekly going to their doom, and the news on the radio, the fact that Joe was dead and he had taken to smoking as readily as if he'd never stopped and ... everything crowded in at once. He couldn't concentrate, could barely think. So much so that he was right on top of a roadblock that stretched fully across the highway before he noticed it. He saw the rifles and hazmat suits too late to be able to turn the pickup around and flee.

Where am I going to go to anyway?

He stopped the pickup and turned off ZZ Top as one of the suited figures stepped up to the window and tapped on it with the barrel of his rifle, indicating that Shaun should wind it down.

He did as he was asked—arguing now was only going to get him shot. He listened though, ready to wind the window up and be damned with it if he heard that drone again. But there was only a thin whistle of wind and the ticking from under the hood as the pickup cooled.

"Please get out of the vehicle, sir."

The voice was polite, almost matter of fact; it didn't even sound like an order, but Shaun was under no illusions on that score. He remembered just in time to take his phone, his smokes and his keys before he was led—not at gunpoint, for the barrel never actually pointed in his direction—over to a long, articulated truck.

"Get in the back, please sir," the suited figure said. Shaun looked in. There were maybe a dozen people inside already, two families at least, and they all looked wide-eyed and shocked—or fearful.

Something prodded Shaun in the back, and he got the message. He clambered up into the back of the truck and sat on the floor, near the door so that he could have a smoke and watch what was going on.

"They're going to kill us, aren't they?" a woman behind him

sobbed. Nobody said anything to contradict her, which only added to Shaun's worries.

Over the course of the next hour the armed men stopped five more vehicles at the roadblock—all of them coming from the west as Shaun had. Three more families and two couples joined the small group in the back of the truck. Then somebody decided they had a full enough load. Shaun just had time to flip the butt of a smoke out the door before it was closed shut on them. The truck started up, and they headed off along the road at speed; they didn't turn so Shaun knew they were still headed east on the highway, and could only guess that Winnipeg might be their destination. He also guessed that he had seen the last of his pickup, for this trip at least.

Nobody spoke, although there were a few whimpers, and some tears. At least the trip was a smooth one—they stayed eastbound on the highway for a while, almost an hour—then the truck lurched as it took a corner too fast, and there was a series of turns after that before they were brought to a halt. The back door rattled open seconds later and Shaun blinked in sudden, bright daylight.

They were let out onto the tarmac of a runway. Somebody had thought this through—they had been brought to an airport. The infection had nowhere to get a foothold on this expanse of gray, and nothing to feed on.

More men in hazmat gear helped them out of the truck, and showed them across the runway and holding bays into the main terminal building of the airport. There were a couple of hundred people already inside, and most of them had the same shocked expression on their faces that Shaun was coming to recognize only too well.

"Coffee and chow is over there," a suited man said, motioning to their left with his rifle. "Make yourselves comfortable— you might be here for a while."

And that was that—no time for questions, no chit-chat, just *sit down and shut the fuck up.* It would be no use trying to argue his way out—all he'd get was shot. These men didn't care that he wanted—needed—to get across the country. They had an infection to control. Shaun understood that at an intellectual level, but at an emotional level he knew he'd need to give vent to some of his frustration soon, before his temper ran ahead of his sense.

Even standing in line to wait for coffee and a sandwich had him ready to climb the walls; and although he saw in the faces around him that many of them felt the same way, it didn't make him feel any better. Becky and the kids were still several thousand miles to the east, but it looked like he'd got as close to them as he was going to get.

16

Rohit managed to keep his charges in check until nearly lunchtime, but the stress of close captivity, coupled with the increasingly dire news on the television meant that something had to give, sooner rather than later. Given the fact that they had only managed some dozed hours of sleep sitting upright in their chairs, it was obvious that the combination of fear, tiredness and frayed nerves would take its toll eventually.

It was the lad who'd smashed his phone—Steve—who cracked first. He didn't give the rest of them any warning. He just stood and headed for the door. Rohit was out of his chair fast, but not fast enough. The door swung open as the youth walked out, just long enough for Rohit to hear a strangely disquieting drone, like a wheezing harmonica, before it swung shut again and the boy was off and away across the car park outside.

Even then Rohit might have gone after him, had he not seen the lad slow, his pace shortening, until he was barely moving. Steve turned almost ninety degrees until he was facing the spot where they'd left the dead girl. Rohit followed the line of his gaze, and saw the oval puffball that had sprouted, dead center, where the girl's chest should be.

Rohit opened the door. The droning got louder, and he felt it tug at him, call him forward. His sight swam, and it was as if he saw something else overlaid on his vision—Blue Hills, and a high plain. He let the door swing shut, and immediately the vision faded, although he knew it would be a while yet before he forgot that sight.

One of the two remaining girls came up behind him.

"What's going on? Get Steve back in here—he'll get himself killed."

Rohit barred her egress with his arm.

"I think it's already too late."

Out in the car park, Steve walked, painstakingly slowly, straight for the puffball, which swelled and contracted at his approach.

"Steve!" the girl behind Rohit shouted, and made a grab for the door again. She managed to get it open a few inches—long enough for Rohit to hear the drone again, and start to feel his head swim. The girl must have heard it too, for she stood back, suddenly confused, and let the door swing shut. By the time Rohit's head cleared, Steve had walked right up to the puffball. His knee touched the crenellated surface; the ball contracted, swelled, then burst at the top, releasing a cloud of spores that hung for a second over Steve's head before falling on his body like rain. Even from across the car park Rohit could see red sores sprout like cartoon measles all across the lad's face and hands. He showed no sign of distress or pain, although he did fall to his knees, as if in supplication before the puffball.

"Steve!" the girl shouted again, but she made no further attempt to reach the door.

They watched in stunned silence as Steve fell forward, face first, into the puffball, sending up another small cloud of spores that rained over him and immediately started to burrow. The youth's legs twitched, twice, then he went completely still.

Rohit turned away, and the girl fell against him, burying her head in his shoulder and sobbing uncontrollably. He could only stand there and hold her, unsure of what to do next, aware that any words of comfort he would be able to muster would most probably ring hollow.

After that the four of them who were left stayed well away from the windows—no one as much as looked in that direction, focusing their attention instead on the television. Watching the mayhem on the news, insulated as it was behind the screen, seemed preferable to looking directly at the stark reality out in the car park.

Although the authorities were trying their best to talk down the severity of the crisis, martial law had been declared in most countries on the planet. The war in the Western Pacific raged unchecked, the equatorial rainforests were brown, squirming with mycelia—and now, everywhere it rained, the puffballs sprung up. And these, more than anything, seemed to be an even bigger cause of worry than the mycelia, for they seemed to be exerting a hypnotic effect on anyone—anything—that came within twenty meters of one.

There were confused reports of drone-like singing, and more about the Blue Hills, but it was obvious that no one, as yet, could make any sense of what was happening. Rohit thought again of the passage in the book he'd read earlier.

On no account should they be cultivated, or allowed to sporulate, for they are voracious in their appetite, and devious in their methods.

Devious seemed to be the appropriate word for what he'd witnessed out in the car park. He looked around at the others. They seemed dulled, listless, as if all fight had gone out of them, and that only made Rohit remember the slow, painstaking way that Steve had walked, straight to his death.

I cannot allow that to happen again.

He also saw one other thing—and it triggered a fresh thought. One of the girls was wearing earphones and listening to music.

Maybe we can blot out the drone, stuff up our ears.

And after that, another thought.

Maybe I can even nullify the drone entirely.

He stood, too fast, knocking his chair over and making everyone jump with a start.

"Sorry, I need to get up to the lab. I have an idea."

Again, nobody volunteered to go with him, but at least they all agreed to keep away from the door—by the looks on their faces he saw that he hadn't had to remind them. He left the three of them around the television and headed back upstairs.

Rohit had known for a long time that different species in the plant kingdom had evolved different methods for trapping prey—from the simple, in the case of sap extrusion in some of the conifers, to the more complicated, like Venus flytraps and some of the sticky marsh worts. Then there was the downright devious, in the pitcher plants that lured insects in the promise of an easy meal, only to trap them and turn the tables in a liquid goop. He hadn't come across any sonic lures in his studies, but that didn't mean that nobody else had ever noted it in the wild. The psychoactive hallucinogen—for that is surely what it must be—was merely an added extra, or so Rohit felt. It was the drone that was the driving force. And now he had a place to start, the old thrill of the quest for knowledge began to override, even if only temporarily, his fear and confusion. There was something here he could focus on, lose himself in, and he fully intended to grab the opportunity.

He had a small library in the lab, but that only had Lloyd's work, *The Carnivorous Plants*, from the nineteen forties, and he already knew that didn't contain what he was after. He went online, and found Darwin's seminal work on insectivorous plants in the 1888 edition, but it still wasn't what he needed. The Germans got him closer. Section five of Karl Goebel's *Pflanzenbiologische Schilderungen* mentioned *the singing fungi of Tibet,* and a name, Catherine Tibbett, a Scottish botanist active in the mid-nineteenth century with whom Rohit was completely unfamiliar. But he had a foothold now, and further digging finally brought him some measure of reward, although in truth there wasn't much more to find.

The details were in a journal published in Glasgow University's Botanical Papers, and were available online through the institution's main library. Ms. Tibbett, the aforementioned botanist, had stumbled across a small population of the puffballs on a remote Tibetan mountainside while searching for a rare magnolia blossom. She had lost three of her guides, and had only survived herself by the simple expedient of stuffing her ears with cotton wool. But, stalwart that she undoubtedly was, she had taken enough time to make detailed notes on the habitat of the fungi and some neat, if somewhat amateurish, drawings, instantly recognizable as being the same as the puffball Rohit had seen outside.

It was her description of the droning song that interested Rohit.

"As I listened closer I heard it, an almost melodious chorus, like a choir of monks heard in the wind."

He also found one other item of note that he thought might be important—the Glasgow Library kept an online record of people who had accessed the document. The last entry on the log before Rohit was for the Chinese Academy of Science, some two years before.

Rohit attempted a search of Chinese records to see if he could find anything else, but either there was no record in English, or all details of their experiments on this particular fungus had already been expunged—Rohit suspected both might be true.

But as he turned away from the laptop, he knew several things he had not already gleaned. The fungus did indeed use some kind of sonic entrapment to catch prey—and the Chinese had most definitely been experimenting on it.

And if they could, so can I.

Getting another sample was going to be tricky, especially as he was going to need to culture one of the puffballs if he was to get to the bottom of the secrets of the sonic drone. But Rohit felt more purpose than he had in the previous twenty-four hours—he had the beginnings of a plan.

He had science to do.

He took a bag containing petri dishes, scalpels, tweezers and gloves back down to the cafeteria, expecting to have to explain himself before he'd be allowed out of the doors—but the three other survivors had other things on their mind. They were clustered around one of the large windows near the doorway, standing, silent, watching something that was going on outside.

"It's Steve. He's still alive," the girl who'd been with Rohit at the door earlier said.

"I doubt that very much," Rohit replied, and stepped forward, only to find a different doubt rise in him. The youth was no longer lying face down in the remains of the puffball. Instead he was dragging himself across the car park—still prone, still face down—and leaving a long brownish smear behind him as he pulled his body across the concrete, heading for the cafeteria door.

"Help him. Please help him," the girl sobbed, but no one moved from the window. Everybody could see that all of Steve's exposed flesh was now a matted, fibrous brown. The infection had him.

It's in charge now, Rohit thought, and realized in the same instant that the thought had more than a hint of truth to it.

"Help him," the girl said again, almost sobbing now.

The crawling figure was only feet away from the door, still face down, still dragging his body along as if it were little more than dead weight.

It's trying to spread itself further. This is behavioral. What the hell did those Chinese do to this fungus to make it so voracious.

He'd never know if he didn't get a sample, and he might never get a better opportunity. Before anyone could notice what he was doing or try to stop him, he opened the door and stepped outside.

Almost immediately he heard the drone again and felt his head spin, but sample taking was something he had plenty of practice in. It only took a few simple movements—a swish of a scalpel, a scoop to get the cut material into a petri dish, and a step back to avoid the crawling figure as it reached for him. He was only outside for ten seconds at most before he stepped back into the cafeteria.

Even then, it took all of his will to close the drone out. Its insidious beat and hum had got into his head, his heart, his bones, and all he wanted to do was go back out and be part of it, to join in its dance, there beneath the Blue Hills. Once back inside he stood there for long seconds, back against the door, waiting for his head to clear and his heart to stop pounding the beat in his ears.

It was only when the others started to scream that he turned back to look outside. The crawling figure had reached the door, and was trying to push it open. Rohit could see Steve's face now—or rather, he couldn't, for there was nothing but an oval ball of matted tissue, brown and somehow dead. The crawling figure slammed hard, twice, against the doorframe, then, seemingly spent, slumped to the ground, leaving a greasy smear down the glass.

Rohit made sure the door was firmly locked behind him, and turned away. The others were trying to talk to him, shouting even, berating him for his stupidity—but Rohit barely heard.

I have my sample. Its secrets will be mine before this day is out.

17

A plant fungus found in the U.K., including a previously found strain affecting resistant wheat varieties, could pose a major threat to wheat production in the country. Using a new diagnostic technique, called field pathogenomics, researchers from the John Innes Centre and The Genome Analysis Centre (TGAC), U.K. found exotic and aggressive strains of the fungus Puccinia striiformis f. sp. tritici (PST) in many counties.

"Yellow rust" caused by the fungus is one of the major diseases affecting wheat crops and is widespread across major wheat-producing areas of the world. Grain quality and yield are significantly lowered by the fungal infection.

New fungus strains that adapt to warmer temperatures have emerged recently.

The song had almost completely captured Jim by mid-morning. He was doing his job well enough that that the men with him in the cleanup crew did not suspect anything untoward. But he was going through the motions much of the time—lost in a reverie on a high plain between Blue Hills, gathering the crop and tending to his fields.

He only came out of it briefly, snatched intervals where he nearly reached lucidity. At those times his arm—the infected one, he knew that much now—throbbed warmly although there was no pain, just a strange sensation of tightness and loss of flexibility that wasn't bad enough to impair his movement. He was also aware that Kerry was watching him closely, although Jim doubted that he was suspected of being infected. If that were the case he'd have been called out on it now, and discarded to his fate like the other poor souls they'd refused to help already that morning.

There seemed to be hundreds, if not thousands of the dead and dying—in the streets, on their porches and gathered in crowds around grocery stores and their parking lots. Fires blossomed everywhere. Jim suspected that many of the afflicted were taking the easy way out. But there were some that looked the way he felt, distracted, as if listening to something, wandering aimlessly on the sidewalks and into the road.

He suspected that the song was calling to them, ever more loudly.

The longest lucid period Jim had that morning was when the truck pulled up in the parking lot of the bigger box stores in Stavanger Drive. The lot itself was empty, save for the dead, of which there were many, and a funeral pyre, still burning, where an attempt had been made, and abandoned, to stay on top of the growing number of bodies.

As they got out of the truck they saw faces pressed against the glass doors of the nearest store—scores of pale, frightened, faces, many of them etched with the telltale tracery of brown filaments across their cheeks. Kerry moved toward the doors.

"Leave them be," Jim said. His voice echoed alarmingly in his head, as if there was far too much empty space in there. It wasn't anything Kerry noticed though. The other man turned.

"We have to help them," he said.

"No. We have to ignore them. You know the orders."

"But they'll die. They'll all die."

"They're dead already, they just haven't noticed yet," Jim replied. "Unless you've found a cure in the past five minutes?"

Kerry looked from the doors, to Jim, and back again.

"But we can't just …"

"We can, and we will. We're looking for survivors, remember?"

"This is bullshit," Kerry replied, but he did turn his back so that he didn't have to look at the anguished faces beyond the glass. "I don't know how much more of it I can take."

"You heard them back at the boat—we're clearing out soon."

"Can't come soon enough."

But when Jim walked across the parking lot towards the store on the other side, Kerry followed him.

Neither of them looked back.

They walked into an empty furniture store. Obviously there was nothing here that any of the survivors—or the infected—needed, and the place hadn't been touched as far as they could see.

"Hello?" Kerry shouted. Again the sound seemed to echo in Jim's head, almost as far off as the now ever-present chanting.

"I'll check upstairs," Jim said, and walked up a dead escalator, his footsteps sounding dull and leaden in the empty space.

The upstairs floor was as empty as the rest of the store, but there were signs that someone had been here—empty snack packets and water bottles on one of the sofas, and a fifth of rum, also empty, on a table.

"Hello?" Jim called, but got no answer.

His arm started to throb again, hotter this time, and painful, like a deep stabbing. His legs threatened to give way under him and he half-walked, half-staggered to the pair of washrooms at the far end of the floor. He caught sight of his face in the mirror as he took off his mask. He was skeletal and drawn, skin too tight over cheekbones that looked like they were trying to escape and eyes sunk like pits, too far back in his skull. He peeled back his glove, got it down to his palm then had to stop, as the material and his skin had become one, fused and woven together by a mesh of the brown filaments. He touched the material at his arm, gingerly, over the original wound. It felt spongy, too loose for healthy flesh. There was a flash of hot pain then, just as quickly, a loud burst of the song and a wash of calm detachment.

Nothing to worry about here—move along now.

He stood at the mirror for long seconds, looking into a face it took him several seconds to recognize. It took him even longer to spot that there was a kid at the cubicle doorway behind him, wide-eyed and staring. His skin showed no sign of any infection.

"It's okay," Jim said, the lie coming far too easily as he turned around. "I'm here to help."

The boy—barely sixteen by the look of him—looked ready to flee at any moment, but Jim was between him and the exit to the washrooms. His gaze went from Jim's face, to the still exposed flesh at his wrist and hand.

"You've got it," the youth said, almost a sob. "How can you be of any help?"

Jim stepped forward, keeping his voice soft.

"We've got it under control," he said. "Antibiotics—you've heard of them?"

He saw hope in the boy's eyes—then killed it as quickly as it had come, swinging a punch with his good hand that knocked the kid first into the cubicle door, then down to the ground where three good kicks to the face left him there permanently. Jim bent, rubbed his exposed infection over what skin he could see, then pulled the glove back up over his sleeve.

"Anybody up there?" Kerry asked as Jim went back down the escalator two minutes later.

Jim shook his head.

"No. Everything's just fine."

18

Rebecca's drive up the island proved to be one long, nightmarish journey through a landscape she barely recognized. She'd lived on The Rock all her life, and thought she knew all of its quirks and ways, its strangeness and charm.

But I've never seen it like this.

At this point in spring the island should be awake, green and vibrant—but everywhere she looked there was only a brown mat of tendrils, and the ever-more-frequent puffballs jutting up into the air. The balls varied in size, from small things barely larger than a hen's egg, to large ovals as tall as a man. The tall ones sent out black clouds of dust high up into the air, mushroom clouds above the mushrooms, rising to scores of feet in height before being dispersed into the wind or falling, like little hard seeds, rattling against the windshield and hood of her SUV.

In the back the boys still seemed oblivious to what was going on outside, still lost, heads down, in their games. Rebecca was thankful for the small mercy.

But how long will the batteries last? How long will we have power to recharge them?

Early in the journey she'd listened to the radio, but after a while she could take no more of the mayhem, destruction, and increasingly scary tales of martial law, looting and wars. The world was going to hell fast—it seemed all it had needed was the little push provided by the fungal attack—mankind was doing the rest just fine all of its own accord.

She had driven in silence as far as the neck of the peninsula and the Whitbourne service station. She'd intended to stop there for gas, but all that stood on the site now was a burned-out ruin surrounded by more of the brown mat, more of the puff-balls, all sprouting from far too many suspiciously human-sized mounds.

The rolling hills up the spine of the isthmus gave her glimpses of what was ahead—more brown, with swirling clouds above laced through with black threads, giving them the look of a chunk of marble, hanging above her, just waiting for the trigger to fall. The sight, and the silence, was too much to bear. She put a disc in the player—one of Shaun's country rock things that she'd always thought innocuous but which now provided a degree of warmth, almost of comfort—and kept her eyes firmly on the road ahead, pushing the accelerator as much as she dared.

There was nothing else moving on the road—no trucks, no motorcyclists—just her and the tarmac.

And so it had gone, for more than two hundred kilometers, all the way up to Clarenville and their turnoff.

It was midday by the time she pulled into the Irving Station, last stop before turning up the Bonavista peninsula towards her childhood home. The gauge was getting low, and her mind was full of the idea that there wouldn't be a station left, that it would be just another burned-out husk, like the one at Whitbourne, and the two at Goobies, that she'd passed on the way up the island.

But she saw it in the distance as she approached—the famil-iar squat building that stood like a gateway to the town itself. There were no other vehicles at the pumps, or in the small car park, but after filling up and making sure the boys were locked in the car, she went inside to pay and was surprised to see a woman behind the counter.

"That'll be sixty-five dollars please, dear," the woman said, and gave Rebecca a smile that didn't quite reach her eyes. She'd been crying—and recently, too, judging by the streaks of mas-cara that ran down her cheeks—but her stare seemed to defy Rebecca to make something of it.

Business as usual—is that the way it's going to be?

Rebecca decided to play along. She passed the woman her credit card.

"Oh, sorry dear, the computer's playing up—probably a fault on the line again, you know what it's like out here on the island. It'll be back soon though, just you wait and see. But have you got the cash?"

Rebecca passed over four twenties. It was as the woman went to the till to make change that she saw what should have been obvious as soon as she entered—thin brown trails ran across the back of both of the woman's hands, disappearing up—and through—the sleeves of the thin cardigan she wore. And now that Rebecca knew what she was looking for, she saw it everywhere. Brown filaments threaded across the sandwiches under the Perspex box on the counter; they ran through the candy bars and chewing gum in the boxes below, and all over the tall cabinet behind the till where the cigarettes were hidden. The brown threads even drifted and wafted inside the cola bottles in the refrigerated unit to Rebecca's right.

The whole place is infested.

Rebecca stepped back, frantically trying to remember if she'd touched anything since coming in. The woman behind the till tried to hand her the change—a ten and a five, both with brown lines, like a child's scrawls, running over their surface.

"Keep it," Rebecca said, and headed for the door.

"I'll put it in the charity box, shall I?" the woman said cheerily. "Some kid might get a new toy out of it."

Rebecca felt gorge rise in her throat as she pushed her way outside, but controlled herself when she saw Adam and Mark at the SUV window.

Just another hundred kilometers—then we'll be safe.

That's what she was thinking as she got back in the vehicle. But she wasn't at all sure she believed it.

The drive up the Bonavista peninsula proved even more of a shock than the highway—at least the main spine road was wide and mostly kept vehicles distanced somewhat from the roadside verges. But now, as she approached her destination, the trees—or what was left of them—seemed to press in around her, as if reaching for the SUV. In some places they overhung the road, dripping globs of moist, greasy, rotted material onto the windshield. She thought the boys were still engrossed in their games but when she checked the mirror she saw two teary faces looking back at her.

"We're in trouble, ma, aren't we?" Mark said softly, and she could only nod in reply—to give voice to her own fear would just scare the boys even more.

"We'll be at the cabin in less than an hour," she said, trying to keep things calm. "We'll be safe there. And dad will be home soon. You'll like that, won't you?"

She got a pair of nods in return.

They're being brave for me.

She felt a swell of pride that, for one joyful moment, over-rode everything else. Then another blob of greasy tissue splattered the glass in front of her, and it was all she could do to keep the vehicle in a straight line as the wipers tried to clear her view through the resultant smear.

Everything on either side of the road was brown, and every-where she looked she saw more of the puffballs. They were taller here than the previous ones, seeming swollen and gorged where they'd prospered on soggier ground.

And it wasn't just the vegetation that had browned. A muddy scum covered the surface of all of the small ponds that lined long stretches of the road, and from these rose an oily haze that danced in rainbow colors, like spilled fuel in sunshine. More black spores fell from above, dancing like tiny bullets off the hood, and higher still the clouds swirled, looming thick and gray and threatening.

Rebecca just had one thought in mind now: get to the cabin on the shore and get inside. Everything else was put to the back of her mind, secondary to that single imperative—so much so that when she passed a vehicle pulled over to the side of the road, and saw a man inside, waving frantically at her, she just put her foot down and kept going. As she passed, he shouted at her—probably an obscenity, given how angry he looked, his face red and livid on one side, and mucky brown and squirming on the other.

By the time she pulled off the road at Melrose and onto the cliff track her nerves were shredded by the strain of the drive, the lowering clouds and the several near misses she'd had while swerving to avoid wrecks or debris that littered the road with dismaying regularity. At least she hadn't had to ignore any more stricken people. Everyone else she had seen was already dead and had turned into little more than a feeding ground for the infection.

In the community of Melrose itself curtains twitched at a couple of the windows as she drove through—at least some folks were still alive—but no one waved her down, or came to their doors, and no one tried to prevent her being on her way.

The cabin, her destination, sat alone on a high, rocky out-crop. It was a terrible spot when the wind got up, but its very remoteness—and the fact that it sat on bedrock, not soil—meant that it had been the obvious choice when she'd thought of a bolt hole. As they approached up the long, gravel drive she saw that the ground to each side was pockmarked with the brown infection; but the house itself sat high and proud on the rock and seemed to be untouched.

For now.

She'd been worried that someone else, someone local, might have remembered the house's unique situation, but there were no other cars at the top of the drive, and the house itself sat, empty and quiet.

Rebecca backed the SUV under the overhang of the car-port—it was old, flimsy and mostly useless in a winter storm but at this moment it provided enough protection from the fall-ing seeds. With one eye constantly on the wind direction she got the kids out of the back and into the house, and lugged all the gear from the trunk into the small hallway before closing the door with a bang behind her.

Well, I'm home.

19

"So, where are you headed?" a voice said to Shaun's left.

He'd been in the airport lounge for three hours now, and his situation hadn't improved any. No planes had arrived or departed as far as he could tell, and the number of people interred in the area was growing steadily.

Through the tall windows he saw fires burning, out past the runways. It was verge clearing, they were told when someone asked; it's body dumps, someone else said after being herded in at gunpoint. The armed, suited figures around the perimeter were getting increasingly nervous, and several scuffles had already been broken up as disgruntled passengers—the word prisoner hadn't been used yet—tried to get out of the lounge and were forcibly restrained from doing so. Tempers were rising—it hadn't been a good idea to start selling liquor—and it was only a matter of time before a full-blown fight got underway.

Shaun turned toward the man who had spoken; he was a small, heavy-set chap in an expensive wool suit, the effect of which was somewhat spoiled by the redness of his face and his tousled hair that stood up on clumps from a thinning pate.

"East," Shaun said in reply. "As far as I can get."

"Me too," the small man answered. "Want to see if we can get there?"

Shaun waved toward the nearest two armed men.

"I don't think they're in any mood to let us."

"Fuck them," the man said, the profanity making him go even redder, as if he'd made a special effort. "There's a door out back in the corridor past the washrooms that nobody's watching. It leads out to the hangers, and I'm willing to bet there's a

Cessna on this field somewhere. If we can find it, I can fly it—
and if I can fly it, I can get us home, or close to it."

"That's a lot of 'ifs,'" Shaun replied.

The small man waved toward the armed men again.

"As many as staying here?" He sat down in the empty chair
on Shaun's left. "You've got kids, right? I can always tell a family
man."

"Two boys—eleven and nine."

"Two girls for me—both in their teens now. And I want to
see them—I need to see them. I can't sit here and let the world go
to shit while my family is out there—God knows where—getting
shat on. Can you do that?"

Shaun didn't have to speak. He was pretty sure the man
would read the answer in his eyes.

The small man nodded, and went on.

"The name's Jim Wozniak by the way—I figure you should
know that, if we're going to do something incredibly stupid
together in the next ten minutes."

"You're a pilot?"

"Well, I can fly. I didn't keep up with the hours to maintain
my license—but yeah, I can fly—if we can find a plane."

"Like you said," Shaun replied. "It's an airport, how hard
can it be?"

"So you're saying you're in?"

Shaun nodded in reply. The decision hadn't been difficult;
inaction was threatening to drive him to distraction, and from
what he saw around him, the armed men's only plan was to herd
people into the lounge and leave them there. Something had to
give, and Shaun was of a mind to make sure that it was under
his terms, rather than those of the men in the hazmat suits.

"What's the plan?" he asked.

Five minutes later Shaun got up, patted Jim Wozniak on the
shoulder as if saying goodbye, and headed for the washroom at
the rear of the lounge. He took the cigarette pack and his lighter
from his pocket—if he was stopped, he would say he was looking for somewhere to have a smoke, which wasn't going to be too
far from the truth anyway.

But no one paid him any heed. The armed guards were too busy with a new influx of people at the main entrance, and Shaun walked right past the washrooms to the door at the end of the corridor. Even then, he expected it to be locked, but someone had been lax in the security arrangements. The door opened out onto a clear expanse of holding bays with a row of hangers some hundred yards away across the tarmac.

They'd agreed on five minutes, so Shaun tried to make himself invisible in the doorway and lit up a smoke. He almost leapt in the air when the door opened at his back, but it was only the small man—Wozniak.

"Any trouble?"

"None, so far. But there's no ride here."

"Let's try the hangars—and we'd best be quick, there's trouble brewing inside."

Wozniak didn't elaborate, but he set off across the tarmac as if he were fleeing for his life. Shaun thought it best to follow.

The small man went straight for the nearest hanger, and Shaun caught up with him just in time to see Wozniak break into a broad smile.

"See—I told you. And these are Mustangs. They'll get us to Montreal before we need to stop." There were four Cessna jets lined up along the left side of the large hangar. "Give me a couple of minutes. I'll check if any are ready to go. Keep an eye out and shout if anyone spots us."

Shaun watched the door to the terminal they'd come through, but there was no sign that anyone had noticed their escape—that's how Shaun was thinking of it; it felt like a prison break, and he was sure there'd be punishment ahead should they be caught.

"Got one," he heard Wozniak shout. He just turned toward the small man when the unmistakable sound of rapid gunfire came across the tarmac—followed immediately by the equally unmistakable sound of panicked screams.

"Time to go," Wozniak shouted.

Shaun walked over to join him.

"We're just going to steal this, right?" he said. "How much is one of these things worth?"

"About three million bucks when new," Wozniak said, and smiled. "Welcome to the big time. Now, are you coming, or do you want to stay here and get shot?"

Shaun followed Wozniak to the furthest jet in line and went up the short set of steps. Once they were inside Wozniak nudged Shaun out of the way to raise the steps up and close the door—also closing out the sound of more, and more rapid, gunfire.

"Most of the comfort is here in the back," the small man said, waving a hand at the cabin. Four plush seats, a small head and even a television set, hung on a hinge from the ceiling so that it could be pulled down for watching. "But I'd like some company up front if you don't mind. I'm not afraid to admit to being a bit spooked by all of this."

"Join the club," Shaun replied, and followed Wozniak up to the pilot's cabin. It too was plush and well appointed, and filled with what, to Shaun's eyes anyway, looked like a bewildering array of knobs, dials, screens and what seemed more like games controls than anything that might be used to fly an aircraft.

"You're sure about this, right?" he said.

The smaller man turned and smiled.

"Please ensure your seat backs and tray tables are in their upright and locked positions. Give me a minute then we can be on our way."

Wozniak took the left-hand seat, so Shaun dropped into the right one. In doing so he looked out of the window and had a clear view out of the hangar door they had come in—and saw two armed men walking across the holding bay from the terminal, coming straight for the hangar.

"It's definitely time to go," he said, trying to keep calm. "We've got company."

Wozniak threw a switch. He put both hands on the controls. With an initial lurch that almost threw Shaun out of his seat, the Cessna rolled forward. The men outside started to run towards the hanger. Wozniak turned the plane till it was facing straight at them, and pushed the throttle, hard.

The left-hand man tried to raise his weapon, but was too slow—he was hit by a wingtip and went down, hard. The other man wasn't even so fortunate, as the front of the fuselage smacked right into him. Shaun saw a spray of blood rise in the air, then felt a bump as the man went under the front wheel.

"Sorry guys," Wozniak said calmly. "I've got a dinner appointment with the wife and kids, and I'm running late already."

Shaun was able to take a look back as Wozniak turned the plane towards the runway. Two bodies lay flat out on the tarmac, and neither moved.

"It was them or us—you get that, right?" Wozniak said as he lined them up and punched the throttle hard enough to force Shaun back in his seat. The small plane roared and bucked, and Shaun's heart leapt to his mouth before, with only the slightest of bumps, they rose up into the air and banked over the airport.

He caught one last glimpse of the two suited men on the ground.

They still weren't moving.

20

Rohit spent the next few hours in his lab, his whole attention on the sample he'd taken from the dead youth in the doorway. At one point the coffee lady—her name was Irene but to Rohit she'd always be the coffee lady—brought him a mug and two cheese sandwiches.

"We have ham but I couldn't remember if you … you know …"

Rohit nodded.

"Cheese is just fine. How are the other two?"

The woman sat down on the stool nearest Rohit, head down, not looking at him as she spoke. It all came out of her at once, as if she couldn't keep it bottled up any longer.

"About what you'd expect, given what's going on. I think they're in shock—I know I am. Frazzled, that's a good word for it. And that poor boy is still slumped against the door—what's left of him anyway—he's all eaten up and sunk in at the chest and …" She had to pause as her breathing decided to catch up with her, and her chest hitched in quiet sobbing before she continued. "And they're saying on the news that anyone who goes outside will be subject to martial law, whatever that means."

"It means you'd probably get shot," Rohit said, his mouth working faster than his brain, and causing the woman's shoulders to slump. She started sobbing more loudly, and Rohit was all too aware of the distance between them. He couldn't comfort her without getting off his own stool, and he wasn't sure he wanted to do that. They sat there awkwardly for long seconds before she fell quiet, rubbed her sleeve over her damp eyes, and sniffed.

"Sorry. I've been trying to keep it together for the kids downstairs but ..."

"... it's hard. I know," Rohit replied. "I've been living on nerves and fumes myself."

The woman—Irene he remembered, again—managed a thin smile.

"We old folks have to stick together."

She motioned at his microscope, and the petri dishes on the right-hand side.

"Have you found out anything—anything that might help?"

Rohit turned back toward the scope. He had indeed found something, but had no clue how to explain it to anyone without using too many overly scientific words, or seeming condescending in over simplifying. His gaze went to the sealed cabinet on the right wall.

"It's probably best if I show you," he said. "Over here."

He was surprised when she took his hand in hers as she walked over to join him, but did not let go. It felt good, natural even. Certainly more natural than the things he had growing in the cabinet.

There were two of them—two small puffballs, each no bigger than Rohit's thumb, one at each end of the cabinet. Despite the fact that the glass was industrial grade and the cabinets well sealed, he still did not venture too close—he'd done so ten minutes before, and the drone had been clearly audible, and powerful enough to set off a dizzy spell. He tightened his grip on Irene's hand and held her away from the glass.

"Best just to look from here. These two grew in less than an hour from some hyphae I put on the substrate."

He saw the first of what he knew might be several blank looks.

"I grew them," he elaborated. "And they grew, too fast for it to be remotely normal. I don't think there's much about this fungus that is natural—I think it was made, designed."

"It's a biological weapon?"

"Well, it is now," Rohit replied, hearing the bitterness in his tone. "I think it might have started out as an attempt to engineer a new, mass-produced foodstuff, but it got out of hand—first in

China, and now, everywhere. But that's not the worst of it."

"There's worse?"

Rohit hesitated. He didn't see how sharing what he knew with someone who was already frightened was going to help, but she deserved to know. Everybody deserved to know.

"I've been experimenting with trying to dampen the sonic drone," he said. "I hoped that I might be able to cancel out its effects on us, at least enough for us to be able to venture outside the building. But it counters everything I do—and comes back with a stronger alternative."

"What are you saying? Are you saying it knows what you're doing?"

"In a sense, yes. It's learning and learning fast. As I said already, this thing was built, not evolved. And it might well have started out as a food substitute, but somewhere along the line someone went a lot further. There's a cell structure in its matrix that looks like nothing I've ever seen before, but I know what it resembles most—ganglion and synapses, nerve clusters and nodules. It looks like brain tissue."

Now that he'd given voice to the thought, Rohit realized how ridiculous it sounded.

"I'm not saying that it thinks," he said.

Irene laughed—he thought there might be just a hint of hysteria in it too.

"I should hope not. But how smart is it. Any idea? Is it like an ant … or a dog?"

Rohit shrugged.

"It's just so different from anything I've ever seen, I can't even begin to guess."

"Why would somebody do such a thing?"

Rohit thought he knew the answer to that one, but *because I could* or *because I wanted to see what would happen* wasn't anything Irene would want to hear. Even then, both those thoughts were preferable to the idea that this was indeed a weapon—something somebody had considered a good idea, until it got out in the wild. Oppenheimer had called himself and his team *destroyer of worlds*. This thing had a chance of doing a better job of it.

He realized that he was still holding the woman's hand, but when he slightly loosened his grip, she held on tighter.

"Does anything you've found out help? Can we stop it spreading? Can anyone stop it spreading?"

"I'm sure there's scientists all over the planet thinking exactly the same thing," Rohit said, with more confidence than he actually felt. "It's just a fungus, after all."

"But is it?" Irene replied. "For what you've told me, this isn't *just* anything."

He had no answer to that.

"I need to keep looking," was all he could say. "There's things I can try, and I need to be doing something."

"So do the kids downstairs," Irene replied. "Is there anything you can get them to help you with to stop them climbing the walls?"

"As long as they have the television, they're better off down there, safer too. I don't know how secure my equipment is against the spread of the infection."

Irene looked shocked at that.

"Then you need to stop. Right now."

"No," Rohit replied, and gently disengaged his hand from hers before turning back toward the microscope. "I need to start … start paying closer attention, and start finding a way of keeping us alive."

21

Jim Noble drifted.

Part of him was aware that he was driving the truck over the Airport Heights road, and another part of him was appalled at a memory of killing the kid in a washroom—although surely that hadn't happened? But most of his attention was on a high plain between Blue Hills under a purple sky.

The crop needed him. It wanted to grow and spread the song. The song was everything and everything was the song.

It was the only thing that mattered.

It was louder now, more confident, with many more voices joined in the choir. Not all could hold a tune, many could scarcely vocalize at all, but the song was the thing and the slow but steady drift of it to fill all the empty places of the world was well underway.

Soon Jim would play his part in that, soon.

But for now he was content to go with the flow.

His head swam, and it seemed as if the scene around him—the truck, the crew, the road ahead—all melted and ran, receding into a great distance until it was little more than a pinpoint in a blanket of darkness. Jim was drifting in a vast cathedral of emptiness where nothing existed save the dark and the song.

He danced.

Shapes moved beside him in the dark, black shadows with no substance, shadows that capered and whirled as the dance grew ever more frenetic; and they joined, two, four, eight, sixteen, ever growing, ever doubling.

They grew. And they danced, there in the dark, danced in time with the song.

They all danced.

Kerry looked askance at him as the truck finally came to a halt at Hamilton Park School Hall.

"You sure you're okay, Jim? You've hardly said a word all day."

Jim waved him away. The right words seemed to come from the darkness, and he spoke without the need to understand.

"I'll be fine. Beer and some hockey will see me all right."

That got a small laugh from Kerry, something else Jim no longer understood. But he knew it was good—he was still not suspected, he was still dancing.

He felt a thrill of anticipation as they approached the main hall. Many had been brought here, many that could be singers, could be dancers. But as soon as they entered and the drone inside him responded in turn he knew. The song was already here, had already been joined. The floor of the school hall was a mass of brown threaded tissue, clumps here and there showing where the singers had joined the throng, the seed bearers grown large and plump and ripe, thrumming and vibrating in time, ready to spread the joy.

He heard Kerry retch and start to weep, but Jim felt no sorrow in this place. They were in the song now.

All were in the song.

All would dance.

22

Rebecca was surprised to find the cabin had both power and water supply. Since her mum passed, they'd only ever used the place as a summer weekend getaway spot, and every year Shaun had to get the local council to switch on the utilities for them in May before their first visit—obviously someone had preempted them this year and done it early. Not that she was complaining; the boys now had the television set on which to play their games. Anything that kept them distracted was fine by her.

She had a working stove, and a shower unit, which she took advantage of as soon as she knew the boys were settled—if not entirely happy. Having the utilities working made her think of Shaun again, but the phones still weren't getting any signal, and the cabin wasn't equipped with an Internet connection, so Wi-Fi was out of the question. She could only trust that he would get her earlier message, and hope that he was indeed on his way.

I don't know if I can get through this without him.

She made herself a mug of coffee and took it over to the picture window, looking out over Trinity Bay to the Atlantic Ocean.

She'd always loved the view.

Shame about the rest of the place.

Growing up she'd hated the very sight of the house. It was too small, too remote, too far from school, too windy—too much of all the wrong things, too few of any of the good ones. She hadn't been able to leave for college in St. John's fast enough, and after she met Shaun her visits home grew few and far between, despite her mother's long protestations at being abandoned.

Now, here she was again, feeling the old nagging guilt but at the same time the all too familiar horror at being so remote from society.

But now, today, maybe that's a good thing.

From the cabin's high spot on the cliff she had a view down a cliff face to a rocky bay, then out to sea. There was no sign of the brown infection in her current field of vision.

She was more than happy for it to stay that way for a while, but her calm was broken almost before she had time to settle into it. The boys had gone quiet—she hadn't noticed, lost in her own reverie, and she only became aware of it when Mark spoke softly, breaking the silence.

"Mum, you need to see this."

She walked round so that she could see where he was pointing at the television. They weren't playing games anymore—although given the carnage on screen, they might as well have been.

It was showing London again, but it was now a city that Rebecca barely recognized. Matted brown filaments ran rampant through streets normally awash with tourists—the fountains in Trafalgar Square were completely clogged, and Nelson's Column was brown and crusted as high as a third of a way up. The Thames had backed up at Hammersmith, dammed with the infection, and overlooked by a small army of puffballs on the bridge above, standing tall and spewing out spores like smokestacks. The pictures were obviously coming in from a helicopter. It banked away from the river and back over Buckingham Palace, which was now little more than a brown, dry mound; over Green Park, a name that would have to be changed; and along an Oxford Street eerily empty and devoid of a single moving soul. St. Paul's, the cathedral that had withstood all that the Germans could throw at it, was a burned-out ruin, the great dome collapsed in on itself and the steps outside festooned, not with tourists, but with tall, silent puffballs. Indeed, the whole city seemed to lie empty, and Rebecca was reminded of those old movies Shaun loved so much, and the quiet, dead streets of the old city that so often heralded an apocalypse.

She got Mark to turn up the volume.

"The pictures you are seeing are not a random, one-off occurrence. Similar scenes are being enacted all across the globe. Where cities are not being engulfed, they are burning, in frantic, mostly futile attempts to contain the menace. But as yet, nothing that has been tried, short of complete destruction by fire, has stopped its spread. The question has to be asked, and we might learn the answer here, right in front of our eyes.

"Is this the way the world ends?"

The picture on screen faded, filled with static, then sharpened again, but didn't seem quite as sharp as previously.

The phones are out, now the television is going. How much longer will we have power?

They'd talked about getting a spare generator for the cabin, but as they were rarely in residence during the worst of the weather, they hadn't got round to doing anything about it. It hadn't seemed urgent at the time. Rebecca spent the next hour taking stock of what they did have in the cabin—apart from what she'd brought in the truck, the small pantry was also pretty well stocked with cans, beans mostly, and dried pasta and rice. As long as the power held out they'd do all right for food. A rummage around at the back of the closet where they kept the activities gear also yielded a small single-burner camp stove and two bottles of propane—Shaun's night fishing supply. She might be able to eke a couple of days cooking out of that—if she was lucky.

The old fireplace in the cabin hadn't seen a flame for as long as Rebecca could remember, but if the power did go she knew she would have to get a fire going—and burn anything that she could get to hand. There was plenty of firewood just outside beyond the drive in normal times; but these weren't normal times, and she wasn't about to risk walking among the infected greenery in search of kindling.

I'll just have to make do.

After her stocktaking, she set to making a pot—a big pot—of potato and meat stew. That way, if the power did go unexpectedly, at least she wouldn't have to start from scratch. As she was chopping vegetables at the table, a vivid memory came to her, of a long-ago winter storm, standing in this same spot as her mother chopped and scraped and filled a pot.

And all of a sudden she was crying, heavy wet tears running down her cheeks.

I'll keep them safe, mum. I promise you, I'll keep them safe.

Once the stew was on and bubbling she made another coffee and joined the boys on the couch. Adam was sound asleep, curled up tight in one corner, but Mark seemed wide awake—even slightly hyperactive, although she sensed that tears might not be far away behind the brave smile he gave her as she pushed him gently aside to make room.

"It's bad all over, mum," he said. "That's Miami—what's left of it."

The screen showed that the infection had run rampant across Florida, eating its way through the vegetation at a prodigious rate and clambering through streets, over buildings, inside houses—driven, so they said, by heat and humidity.

At least we don't have to worry too much about that here on The Rock in April.

And it seemed there was something new to report, something so strange that it took her a while to process the import of it. Again she recognized the city—Edinburgh Castle is hard to mistake—but what she didn't understand at first was the sight of what looked like black beach balls rolling down the cobbles of the Royal Mile. As the camera zoomed in she saw that the balls weren't black at all, but brown, and crenellated. They burst on impact with anything they touched—lampposts, vehicles, and people. The camera cut away as one of the balls bounced, then hit a running man hard in the back. Then, rather than exploding, it opened out, a black crow at the man's neck, before clasping shut, tight on the screaming mouth, cutting off the sound. The last thing the camera caught was the figure falling, pole-axed, and another ball bouncing and unfolding on top of his prone body. His legs kicked twice, then went still.

As the report cut to a talking head, Mark finally asked the question she knew had been worrying at him all day.

"Do you think Dad's okay?"

She put her coffee down on the small table and pulled the boy close. He was at an age now where he'd normally complain and move away, but not this time. She felt him sob, just once, against her shoulder.

"He texted, said he's coming home. And you know your dad. If he says it, he means it. Just you wait and see. He'll be here as soon as he can. I'm sure of it."

As she said it, Rebecca realized something else. She believed it. Shaun would be doing everything in his power to make it back to them—that was his job.

And it's my job to make sure we're all in one piece when he arrives.

23

There was only so much of the view from the cockpit that Shaun could take. They'd been in the air for well over an hour now, and everything they could see below them was brown and infected, with only small patches of green still showing. Fires sent tall plumes of smoke high into the air above many towns and settlements, and Wozniak was forced to fly low to keep below the heavy, spore-filled clouds that loomed above. Everything had an air of doom and death, and Shaun found himself thinking more and more of the two men they'd left lying on the tarmac. It seemed Wozniak might have been thinking along similar lines.

"See if there's any booze in the back, would you?" the small man said. "My nerves are shot, and this seems like the kind of crate where the owner would have some decent liquor aboard."

Shaun took the opportunity to go back into the passenger cabin and light up a smoke, sucking it down and trying to find a spot of calm. The small plane bucked and swayed in ways he wasn't used to, each lurch bringing with it the worry of plunging out of the sky.

Yep—a drink would go down just fine right about now.

He finished the smoke and did some searching, finding a fridge and drinks cabinet behind the rearmost seat. There was an almost full bottle of single malt Scotch, and he took it and a couple of glasses back up front.

"We need to talk about our plan," Wozniak said as Shaun poured them both stiff measures.

"We have a plan?" Shaun replied, only half-joking.

"'Get to Montreal, fill up, and head for Moncton,' is mine,

but I'm guessing from your accent that you're from The Rock. Is Moncton good enough for now?"

Shaun nodded.

"It's a start. I can get a ride and head up through Prince Edward Island—hope a ferry is running, or charter a boat."

"Or steal one ..." Wozniak added, and Shaun nodded again.

"In for a penny, in for a pound. It's not as if anyone is paying attention."

They'd been listening on the radio, expecting someone, anyone, to contact them, threaten them. But there had been nothing. It seemed they had got away and clear.

Better than those two we left on the tarmac anyway.

He pushed that thought away; his focus had to be ahead, not behind. Wozniak was talking, and Shaun had missed a bit—something about an airfield.

"... Montreal is too big, but there's a small field that fishermen use to get in and out of the wild. I've been there twice. The strip's long enough for us to land this crate just fine, and there'll be less chance—I hope—of anyone trying to stop us."

"Whatever you say, pal," Shaun relied. "You're the boss."

He eyed the Scotch bottle again—the temptation to get lost in its depths was large—but he'd need a clear head. He had a feeling that refueling wasn't going to be quite as simple as Wozniak might like it to be.

Twenty minutes later they were making a wide circle over a small provincial airfield.

"I don't see anybody," Wozniak said. "Do you see anybody?"

All Shaun saw was brown where there should be green. It looked like all the vegetation was infested. Forest, grass, shrub and cropland, even the ponds and lakes were all gray, sepia tinged, and lifeless.

"We can't land here," Shaun said. "It's not safe."

"Could be worse," Wozniak replied and let out a laugh that had little humor in it. "It could be raining."

He lined the Cessna up with the runway and brought her down into a slightly bumpy but safe enough landing, before taxiing over toward the small group of buildings that denoted the administrative area and hangars.

"Over there," he said after a few minutes. "There's the pumps. I'm going to get as close as I can, then make a dash for it—I should be able to stay under the wings if I do this right. I'll need you at the doorway, keeping an eye open. And don't worry, big man. This is the last lap—get this done and in five minutes we'll be on our way back East, and home for supper."

Everything fell suddenly quiet when Wozniak cut the engine. And it was just as quiet outside when they opened the cabin door and let down the steps. The air smelled of damp and rot, and Shaun was suddenly reminded of the scene at the logging camp.

"Five minutes, right?"

Wozniak patted him on the arm and left the plane, heading under the wing to a fuel hose that snaked across to the nearest hanger.

"Just keep an eye open, and shout if anyone looks like bothering us."

Shaun took the opportunity to light up another smoke as Wozniak hooked up the fuel line. At least the taste of it masked the dank smell, but a feeling of deep dread seemed to creep all around him, sinking into him. And now there was something else—a droning hum, distant, but getting definitely louder. He started to walk toward the sound before his head caught up with his body and forced it to a stop.

"There's something funky going on here," he said, and his voice seemed to echo in his head, as if he had a cold coming on.

"I feel it too," Wozniak called out. "Hold on, we've got fuel going in. We're nearly there."

The drone got louder, and Shaun's head swam. The last time he'd felt anything like it had been on going under anesthetic for dental surgery, but this was different. This felt guided somehow, purposeful. Then he remembered the animals crossing the highway, and the sound outside the pickup.

He stepped quickly back inside the plane, which dampened the effect slightly, at least enough for him to shake it from his head.

But Wozniak is still outside.

Moving quickly, he took a bundle of tissues from the top of the drink cabinet and stuffed them, hard, in his ears. The drone cut off, its effect nullified.

But for how long?

Taking another handful of the tissues he went back outside. Wozniak had walked away from the plane, his eyes glazed, heading across the runway, straight for the brown verge beyond. Shaun caught up with him five yards from the edge of the tarmac, and turned him around. There was no recognition in the man's eyes, and he immediately tried to turn away again, attempting to squirm from Shaun's grip.

It took three attempts to get the tissues wadded in the smaller man's ears, but almost immediately after that his eyes cleared, and he shook his head, as if clearing it.

"Back to the plane, quick," Wozniak shouted. Shaun didn't hang around to disagree, but when they turned they saw that they were no longer alone on the tarmac.

A man stood at the foot of the plane's steps.

He had a gun pointed straight at them.

The gun was the first thing Shaun saw; the second was that the man was clearly infected. He wore earplugs—the small, personal ones, so immune to the sound of the drone—but it was too late for him anyway. Brown filaments ran across both cheeks and tugged at the left corner of his mouth, making it droop like he'd suffered a stroke. His eyes were clear though, and his voice carried loud enough even through the wadded tissues.

"I'm coming with you."

Seeing the size of the gun—it was a handgun, but the barrel looked like a bloody cannon—Shaun was inclined to acquiesce, but Wozniak had other ideas.

"Can't do that, man," he shouted, shuffling forward, never taking his eyes off the weapon. "I've got my wife and kids to think of. We're still clear, we're not infected."

"I'll shoot," the man replied, and aimed straight at Wozniak.

"Then who'd fly you out of here?"

The gunman seemed momentarily confused by the question, and his hesitation gave the small man the opening he needed. Wozniak launched himself at the armed man, head down in a shoulder charge that sent them both sprawling on the tarmac. The gun went off, the shot loud even through the tissues in Shaun's ears.

"Get the gun," Wozniak shouted, and finally Shaun moved to his aid. He stepped forward and stomped down on the armed man's wrist, twice, feeling bone give way before the weapon fell from his grasp. Wozniak lifted the gunman's head from the tarmac and slammed it down hard, then again. The back of the skull gave way and the man fell back, suddenly still. There was almost no blood, and what little there was looked brown and watery.

Shaun bent to retrieve the gun.

"Leave it!" Wozniak shouted. "He touched it. It might be infected." The small man left Shaun standing over the body, went under the wing and disengaged the fuel line. "Let's get the flock out of here before somebody else comes along."

As he followed Wozniak back into the plane Shaun saw the small man wince, grab at his side, and bring a bloody hand away.

"Bastard nicked me—don't worry, I'll be fine. Let's get the bird up first, then we can worry about it."

Shaun waited until they were back in the plane with the door firmly shut before removing the tissues from his ears. The drone had gone again, leaving just a memory, a promise of peace and rest that was still somehow beguiling. Without the wadding, Shaun knew he'd have given in to its call, and gone gladly.

He followed Wozniak into the cockpit. The small man winced in fresh pain as he sat down, but waved Shaun away.

"I said, let's get her up first—I'll be happier when we're in the sky. But first, get the Scotch."

"Should you be drinking?"

"It's not for drinking, you idiot. I touched that fucker. Who knows what I got on me? Pour it over my hands—and quick—time is probably of the essence."

Shaun did as he was told. The cockpit filled with the high smell of the liquor as Wozniak rubbed it into his hands and wrists, then took to the controls. As he kicked in the engine and they started to roll away, Shaun saw movement at the edge of the runway, although at first he didn't believe what he was seeing. Black balls rolled out of the verge—they were the size of soccer balls and bigger—and unhesitatingly made straight for the prone body the men had left behind. As Wozniak took them off and away, Jim just had time to see the first ball open out, like an actor opening a cape with a dramatic flourish, then swoop down over the dead man, who was quickly, and thankfully, lost from sight.

The first traces of brown filament appeared in the wound in Wozniak's side twenty minutes later.

24

Rohit knew there had to be something he was missing. Many plant species have natural chemical defenses against fungal attacks, but from what he'd seen on the news and read online, this newest invader was riding roughshod over all of them. Rohit had tested some of them himself on his sample—nicotine infusions, coffee, pyrethin-based mold remover, and several common disinfectants based on pinesap extract. The new fungus ate them all up and came on for more. It seemed the organism had been built with a prime directive that overrode everything else.

If it's organic, it's dinner.

But while considering the fact that the thing had been made in a lab, cobbled together from bits and pieces, Rohit had what proved to be an epiphany. The bundles of tissue that looked like neurons had to have come from somewhere, a building block that had an origin. And if was indeed nervous tissue, then maybe it wasn't a defensive strategy he should be considering; maybe it was an attacking one. He stopped researching plant defenses and began looking into neurotoxins.

He was aware he was straying outside his own, admittedly narrow, field of expertise, but he felt rising excitement and anticipation—he was onto something, something that was confirmed when he read about the psychoactive effects of some neurotoxin transmitters.

That's how they're producing the visions. It must be.

His research was leading him down some strange pathways, and he had to laugh when Irene brought him coffee and, when asked what he was reading, he was able to reply, with a straight face, "The effects on brain chemistry of licking the Sonoran Desert toad."

The more he read, the more he was convinced he was on the right track.

But how am I supposed to test it?

It wasn't as if he had a ready supply of neurotoxins at hand. Then he remembered that he had plenty of one of the simplest of all, one all labs have in supply. He retrieved a bottle of ethanol and took it over to the cabinet. Opening it only as far as he dared—even then the sound of the drone and the light-headed effect kicked in immediately—he poured fifty milliliters or so over the top of the rightmost puffball.

The effect was immediate. The fungus shrank and fell apart into a mass of slimy goop that hissed and steamed. There was another effect he hadn't anticipated. The second puffball, clear across the cabinet, also shrank and contracted down to little more than a hard nodule of the mycelium. Although it did not lose cohesion and fall apart, it also showed little sign of putting up another puffball. When Rohit tentatively opened the cabinet, there was no recurrence of the drone, nor any associated light-headedness.

I may have found our weapon.

He didn't even have time to get excited—at that very same instant, the power failed and he was left sitting in the gloom as the sun went down outside the windows.

25

The thing inside Jim Noble's hazmat suit hummed to himself as he worked. What little remained of Noble was buried in there somewhere, somewhere deep, but he was long past caring, lost to the song. He knew enough to function, to not draw attention to himself, biding his time until … he wasn't quite sure. But waiting was what was needed, he knew that part well enough.

So he waited.

Kerry spoke to him from time to time, and he spoke back, most of the right words, mostly in the right order.

They'd burned the school—all of it, all the way to the ground. They'd also burned the Avalon Mall, St Peter's Church Hall, three gas stations and two Tim Horton's drive-ins. The fires no longer bothered Noble. The song had already been joined, the dance was growing faster than ever, so some smoke and flame did little to stop what was coming. His anticipation was growing and he had to calm himself—he could not give himself away now. His turn would come. The wait was almost over; he could feel it.

Soon.

It will be soon.

26

Although she wasn't to know it, Rebecca lost the power to the cabin at the same time as Rohit was plunged into darkness. The boys wailed in misery as their current game on the big screen went black. After several minutes of rushing about, getting candles and a fire lit, the three of them sat around the old table eating the stew that she'd kept bubbling on the stove.

Her youngest, Adam, was still silent and withdrawn, replying only in monosyllables when she asked him anything. The power outage seemed to be the last straw for the boy, and after eating he went back to being curled up in the corner of the sofa, as if believing he might be able to wake up and it would all have been a dream.

If only it were that simple.

Mark also sat on the sofa. He had his tablet on, playing a game with the screen light turned right down, trying to squeeze maximum use out of what battery power he still had. That reminded Rebecca about the phone—she should get it charged up from the car charger, just in case Shaun managed to get through.

But that means going outside.

She bit the bullet. It was going to be full dark in less than half an hour, and better to do it now than later, when she would barely be able to see her hand in front of her face.

"Where you going, Mum," Mark said, although he never looked up from the game.

"Out to the car. Need to charge up the phone, and I'll check the radio—see if there's any news on the outage."

That seemed to placate Mark enough, as he was already back

at the game before Rebecca reached the door. She had no real hope of good news about the outage. Outages were a common enough occurrence on The Rock in winter, but mostly unheard of after the snow had gone. And when she looked out the door and across the bay, where they'd normally see the lights of towns on the Carbonear Peninsula, there was only gathering darkness and heavy swirling cloud.

There was also the drone, the same low hum, getting ever stronger, but at least she could block that from her mind by the simple expedient of getting in the car, turning on the engine and switching on the radio while the phone charged up.

The news was all of the bad kind, and there was not much of it, for many stations were broadcasting dead air. She finally found one in English on the Long Wave that was faint, but audible

"It is estimated that the scourge now covers forty per cent of the globe, and its reach is expanding exponentially. As yet none of our attempts to stop its march have met with any success. The great cities of the world are falling into anarchy and chaos, our farmlands and forests are dead and infected, and our people have become just so much food for this invader. Governments are calling for calm in the face of the disaster, but as the song grows louder and the Blue Hills become closer and clearer, survival can be the only thing on the minds of anyone listening to this broadcast. May God be with you and yours, on this, our darkest day."

Well, that's cheered me up nicely.

Rebecca wished she still smoked; a cigarette and a drink sounded damn fine right around now. The phone beeped, and she grabbed for it.

Shaun!

But it was a reminder from their supplier to top up their minutes. It seemed the end of the world wasn't enough to stop automated systems sending annoying messages.

The thought struck her as funny, and she laughed. Once she'd started, she couldn't stop, although it quickly turned to tears and weeping that lasted until the phone beeped again, telling her it was fully charged.

She wiped her eyes, checked in the mirror that she didn't look too teary or disheveled, and, humming loudly to mask the drone, quickly made her way back into the cabin. By the time Mark looked up at her entrance, she was Mum again, and ready for whatever might be thrown at her next.

Adam woke up soon after that, and they spent the evening playing board games—there was an old box in the dresser that had been there since Rebecca played them with her Grandma, some twenty-five years before. She had to teach the boys the rules for most of them, physical game-playing being a lost art to them. But they soon got into the swing of things, and they were quickly lost in the competitions, so much so that Rebecca even manage to forget about their situation for minutes at a time, carried away by older, more simple, pleasures as candlelight flickered across the rolling dice.

It was a moment of complete nostalgia that threatened to overwhelm her emotions; her Grandma's presence felt almost close enough to touch. But all that was all too quickly shattered; the golden moment ended when something hit the roof of the cabin, hard enough to shake the frame of the dwelling and rattle the big window.

Adam immediately left the table and went to huddle up in the corner of the sofa again, his head buried in the large cushion on the corner. Mark stood to be at Rebecca's side.

"What is it, Ma?"

They waited for a recurrence—but none came. Outside the big window there was only blackness, but as Rebecca turned she saw a flickering from through in the kitchen, a dancing aura of color outside the window there. When she rose to go to investigate, Mark came with her, taking her hand and walking by her side.

The kitchen window looked south, over the rocky cliffs that ran away into darkness. The dancing light came from the rough vegetation that topped the rock, shimmering and cavorting as if alive in a rainbow of swirling color that spun around three tall ovals that could only be more of the puffballs. As Rebecca and Mark watched, a breeze came up. The central puffball opened out, spreading thin wings that spanned several meters across, and with the next gust took flight, soaring up and over the cabin, as smooth and quiet as a huge manta ray cruising through black ocean depths.

27

"I'm not going to make it."

Shaun could only agree with the prognosis. The brown filaments at Wozniak's wounded side were now knitted around the wound, through flesh and clothing and even into the fabric of the seat itself, effectively sewing the small man to the chair. The booze seemed to help when applied both internally and externally—Wozniak was certainly more aware and awake than Shaun might have expected. But it had become increasingly obvious that the infection was winning whatever battles were being fought in the war for his body, and his mind.

"I can hear it, you know?" Wozniak said, tapping at his skull. "I can hear it singing to me, and see it too. Blue Hills and a high plateau, and the gardeners tending to the crop under a purple sky."

He turned to Shaun, and repeated himself, as if trying to believe it.

"I'm not going to make it."

"So what's the plan?" Shaun asked. He was sitting as far back in his chair as he could, keeping distance between himself and the pilot. For all he knew he was already infected himself.

But it's not as if I can get out and go somewhere else.

"I'm not going home," Wozniak replied. "I can't bear the thought of them seeing me like this. But we can get you close to yours. I diverted our flight path a while back, and we've just about got enough fuel to make it—I'm heading for Gander—then you're on your own."

"I'm not leaving you."

"I don't think you'll have a choice by then. But first, let's just concentrate on getting that far. Pass the Scotch. That blasted singing is getting too loud again."

Wozniak had already drunk enough to floor a horse, but he seemed lucid and almost calm, far calmer than Shaun would have been under the circumstances.

"Get any smokes left?" the smaller man asked as he passed the bottle back. "I'm ten years and more quit, but one now isn't going to make any difference to my life expectancy."

"We could land—look for help?"

Wozniak waved at the view out of the window. It was almost dark outside. Few of the towns and cities they passed still had power, and what little they could see of the land below was punctuated with fires.

"I think we're better off up here, don't you?"

Shaun lit up two cigarettes and passed one over, taking care that he didn't come into any contact with the other man.

"Maybe you should get in the back and close the door," Wozniak said. "It might be safer that way."

"I said, I'm not leaving you."

"It might be your funeral," Wozniak replied.

"And it might not. I sat in a car with an infected friend yesterday morning and I'm still here. I'm not about to abandon another."

"You know, I think we could have been at that—friends I mean, in another lifetime."

Shaun nodded.

"Just hold that thought. They might have figured out a cure by now ... there might be help at the airport. Maybe ..."

"Ifs and buts, maybes and possibilities ... it doesn't make any difference," Wozniak said, and tapped his head again. "I'm too far gone. I can feel it in here, singing and whispering. It wants me to come over there and make you join us—that's how it thinks of itself, some kind of huge collective. Looks like the Commies have finally won."

He laughed, coughed, and spit up blood on the controls in front of him.

"Not long now. Best give me more Scotch. It's the only thing keeping me going."

He lasted almost another hour—just about as long as the last of the Scotch. Shaun had been staring out the window at the black night beyond, his mind racing with worry.

"We're over the St. Lawrence Bay," Wozniak said softly, the first time either had spoken for twenty minutes. "I'll be descending, then the fun will start."

"More fun? Wonderful."

Wozniak laughed, and spat up more blood.

"We have to hope that the runway is lit at the airport; if not, we'll be going down blind, and that's not going to end well."

"Great. Something to worry about. I needed that."

Wozniak smiled thinly.

"Buckle up. It could be a bumpy ride."

They started their descent in almost pitch darkness. There were several communities below them as they reached The Rock, large ones that Shaun knew well, but there was no light from any of them, and Shaun's worries grew even larger as they approached Gander. He almost let out a cry of relief when he saw the landing strip lined up straight ahead, leading them down.

"We're going to make it," he shouted.

"Well, one of us is," Wozniak said, and coughed. A sheet of blood ran down his chest, and he slumped alarmingly before an effort of sheer will shot him back upright.

"See you on the other side, pal," he said, and put the plane into a steep descent that felt too fast, too soon. Shaun could only hold on and pray as they plunged out of the sky.

They hit the ground hard, too hard, for something seemed to lurch and tear in the undercarriage. They bounced, and on the second touchdown Shaun's side of the plane collapsed. The wing scratched along the tarmac in a shower of sparks, then was torn off completely, the force of it turning the plane in a slow spin that was taking them, careering, still too fast, toward the end of the runway.

It was only a retaining pile of sand that stopped them from carrying straight on toward the road that bounded that side of the field. But the sand trap did its job and the plane finally came to a shuddering halt.

"We did it. We're down," Shaun said.

But Wozniak hadn't made it with him. The smaller man sat, hunched over the controls. Fresh blood, brown and watery, ran down from his mouth, and his torso was too thin, sunken at the chest. He was clearly dead, but as Shaun undid his seat belt, Wozniak's mouth opened, and the drone-like singing started up, loud and ringing in the confines of the cockpit.

Shaun fled, out through the cabin and out the door, almost falling face first on the tarmac in his haste to escape. There were lights in the distance, a possibility of human contact.

He headed for them, and he didn't look back.

Any hope he had of finding company was quickly quashed. He reached the main building with no mishap, and the sight of lights inside sent his hopes even higher. But the whole facility seemed to be empty. Thankfully there were no bodies, no sign of infection, and the hum of the generators told him that some-one had at least switched on the auxiliary power at some point. But after five minutes' exploration he was forced to admit that the airport had been cleared. And it had been done forcibly, for there was blood on the floor, and spatter on the doors, in three different places, and it looked like there had been a prolonged bout of gunfire, judging by the holes in some of the walls and the spent casings on the ground.

They'd left in a hurry too—the vending machines hadn't been emptied. Shaun took the opportunity to stock up, filling his pockets with candy bars—empty fuel, but fuel nonetheless. He also raided the small shop on the concourse for fresh smokes and a pack of lighters from behind the counter.

The empty quiet of the building was starting to prey on his nerves, and his worry for Becky and the kids was, if anything, stronger now that he was so much closer to home. He left the concourse and headed for the parking bays out front of the ter-minal, in search of a ride that would get him up the coast to his family.

This time his luck was in. The parking lot was bare save for three pickups, but two of those still had keys in the ignition. He was just about to get into the one with the most fuel when he heard the drone again—faint, as if far off, but insistent, demanding his attention. He stepped up into the pickup and reached to pull the door closed. Something hit the roof of the truck, hard, and slid off. As the door shut with a click Shaun was aware of something—several things—fluttering across his field of view. At first he took them for crows, but they soared rather than flapped, almost like black scraps of paper, and moved silently, gliding with the wind, off to Shaun's right and out of sight in the dark. He sat there for several seconds, lighting up a fresh smoke, and only drove off when he was sure he wouldn't be impeded.

It was more than a two-hour drive to Becky's mum's place up on the peninsula—it was going to feel like the longest two hours of his life.

28

Rohit and the three other survivors sat huddled in the cafeteria kitchen. Irene had soup bubbling on the propane stove, and they had enough candles to give them light for the night, but Rohit knew that, come the morning, decisions were going to have to be made. They had only a small supply of fuel and precious little food—the cafeteria was due a delivery, but nobody was holding their breath waiting for one.

The students persisted in attempts to use their phones, but all they succeeded in doing was running down their batteries. Nobody got a signal, nobody took a call or a text.

The rest of the world could be gone, and we'd never know it.

There was also the infection to worry about.

At the moment the lights had gone out up in the lab, and before Rohit found his small flashlight, the cabinet's battery powered fail-safe had kicked in, thinking an emergency had occurred. Air swirled and sucked behind the glass as it was vacuumed away—and something responded, fluttering and knocking like a trapped bird. Rohit's flashlight beam caught it just before it too was sucked away. The remaining puffball, opened out with wings extended, slapped twice on the glass before disappearing from sight.

Flight. It has taken flight. What in hell's name did the Chinese make?

At least they knew how to defend themselves—at least partly. Rohit had fetched two gallons of ethanol down from the lab and swabbed down the area immediately around the main door just before they had all adjourned to the kitchen.

Thinking about that reminded him it was time to check

on the situation, for the power had been out for almost three hours now. He left the others huddled around the stove—no one remarked on him leaving—and went through to the main cafeteria.

He saw immediately that the situation was even worse than he could imagine.

It wasn't dark outside the main windows that looked across the parking lot; the view was filled with dancing shimmering aurora of light, greens and blues and yellows that in other circumstances might even be thought beautiful. It could only be coming from one thing, the infection itself. As Rohit walked towards the doorway he saw that it too was giving off the luminescence—only from the outside though, for it seemed that the ethanol was indeed keeping the thing at bay.

But for how long?

And now that he was close to the doorway, Rohit heard the humming drone again, felt it tug at his mind, even stronger now than before. He backed away, his head spinning and dizzy. He had to take five long steps backward before it cleared.

We're trapped. We can't go out, not into that.

Irene looked up as Rohit returned to the kitchen, and without being asked, handed him a mug of coffee. As she did so, she put a finger to her lips. He knew what she was saying.

The kids can't handle any more bad news at the moment.

As he sat down next to Irene, Rohit also realized that he was dog-tired. He'd slept barely three hours in the last forty, and it was starting to catch up on him fast. The coffee was strong enough to give him a temporary jolt, but he'd need sleep sometime soon, otherwise things would start to get fuzzy. Mistakes might happen, and in their current situation, nothing good would come of it.

The other two girls seemed whipped. They were dozing fitfully, heads down.

Lost. They've lost their anchors and are just drifting.

Rohit understood the feeling intimately—he'd felt that way a lot since coming to North America, and it was his work that rooted him in place. And now even his science was going to be taken from him, as the infection was clearly winning, adapting far faster to circumstances than any defense mankind could put up. Once again he wondered exactly what the Chinese had been up to, for he was sure now that this was no foodstuff experiment gone wrong. This seemed deliberately induced. The only question was a moot one: was it a planned attack on the world, or was it a lab error gone catastrophically wrong? It didn't matter which. It was out, and it had a whole world to conquer.

Look on my works ye mighty and despair.

He was surprised to be shaken awake at some point later—the coffee obviously hadn't been quite strong enough and he'd fallen into a doze. He came up out of a dream of Blue Hills and purple sky to see Irene, wide eyes and afraid, saying something it took him a while to process.

"There's something going on outside, several trucks and bright lights. The other two have gone to check. They've gone outside. The kids have gone out."

As he stood, groggily at first, and needing Irene's help to get his balance, he heard an amplified voice calling.

"Come on out and show us your face and hands. We're here to help."

The cavalry has arrived.

The main thing Rohit remembered later of the next half-hour was the overwhelming smell of industrial alcohol—he hadn't been the only one to make the connection with nerve agents. They were stripped and hosed down in the back of a long truck, given earplugs to combat the drone, and overalls to wear that also reeked of alcohol. Their rescuers, all masked and all wearing earplugs making conversation impossible, checked them over once again for infection, then they were transported slowly, still inside the truck, for about twenty minutes.

Nobody spoke, and Irene held tight to Rohit's hand all the way.

They were let out onto a floodlit dock at the harbor, and then up a gangway into the hold of a boat, where around twenty other overall-clad people wandered, somewhat aimlessly. None of them wore earplugs, so Rohit took his out, and put them away in a pocket.

"So what's the idea here?" Irene asked as she took out her own plugs. "Are we prisoners?"

One of the suited figures walked over to them.

"There's coffee and pizza over at the sharp end," he said. "You're safe here—for now at least."

"Where are we?" Irene asked.

"The *Tealady*—sorry, the *Sea Princess*—usually a supply boat for the oil rigs. It's been press ganged into service."

"Supply boat? We have lots of food and water available then?"

"Yes, ma'am, no worries on that score. Now make yourselves at home. You're the last aboard and we'll be underway any minute now."

"Where are we heading?"

"North," the suited man replied.

Rohit had too many other questions—so many that he couldn't formulate a single one of them—and the man had moved on before he could speak. He let Irene lead him forward to where a queue snaked back from a makeshift food counter. As they waited, he looked up; the closed doors of the cargo bay were fifteen feet or so above them.

Sealed in a metal container. That's probably the best outcome we could have hoped for.

He saw the surviving students from the cafeteria run across the hold and embrace an elderly couple.

"You got us through it," Irene said.

"I didn't do anything," Rohit replied, which earned him a firm squeeze on his hand.

"In that case, just keep on doing nothing," she replied. "I feel safe being with you—if you don't mind?"

Rohit found that he didn't mind at all.

29

It was almost time.

Noble and Kerry had boarded the *Sea Princess* with the last of the folks brought down from the University. Kerry had been prepared to take the truck back out again, but the order came in—they were to stay on board, and head north with everyone else—the town—the whole island—was being abandoned to the fungus.

As Noble passed the radio room he heard a broadcast going out, for stragglers to head up the coast to Carbonear, Bonavista and Twillingate, where attempts would be made to pick them up where possible.

More partners for the dance.

He'd also overheard the conversation between the two they'd brought in from the university, and Kerry.

"We have lots of food and water available then?"

"Yes, ma'am—no worries on that score."

Noble stood silently in a corner of the hold watching the snaking line that waited for food, waiting for the boat to move under him, waiting for the sign that would tell him it was time for him to move.

Time for him to dance.

30

Rebecca finally got the kids to sleep around ten—there was still no sign of power returning, and neither of the boys would go to the back room, so she bedded them down on the sofa with whatever cushions and duvets that came to hand.

As for herself, Rebecca felt bone tired, but her brain refused to shut down. The last thirty-six hours had taken on the feeling of a nightmare, something that had happened slightly remote from reality.

Surely the real world isn't so breakable, so easily unwound?

Sitting in the candlelit cabin, with all technology stripped away, Rebecca felt as close to her childhood—to her mother—as she had for many years—as close, and yet as far away as ever. She missed Shaun with an ache deep down inside her, a fluttering in her stomach and tightness in her chest that was almost unbearable. If it hadn't been for the boys she would, long ago, have gone in search of a bottle.

When she got up and went to make more coffee to try to stave off the urge for booze, she caught another glimpse of the view out of the kitchen window, and was glad there was no liquor in the house, for she might have dived straight in.

The colors still flowed and surged out there in the darkness—a swirling phantasmagoria that was strangely hypnotic and compelling, calling her outside where there would be peace, and rest, and never anything else to worry about again. She left a mug of coffee on the counter and was headed for the door before she caught herself in the act.

Her mind cleared when she dragged herself away from the window—it appeared the light show was almost as compelling as the droning song had been earlier. Keeping her head turned to one side she drew the thin curtain over the scene—it didn't blot out all of the dancing lights, but at least it did enough to keep her from answering its call.

It also darkened the room considerably, so much so that when she turned back to the main living area she was able to see that they were no longer alone in the cabin. Adam still lay curled up, swaddled in blankets in the corner of the sofa. But Mark had adopted his usual position—half in, half out, with his right hand dangling, almost touching the floor.

Rainbow color, faint but unmistakable, danced just beneath his drooping fingers. As Rebecca walked over, slowly, not quite believing what she was seeing, she was able to make out the fine, almost hair-thin tendrils, stretching up from the floorboard, tasting the air as if in anticipation of the flesh now only millimeters above.

She scared the boys again—she had to do it to get them awake and moving, but that didn't mean she was happy about doing it. She hurried them out to the car, and turned the music system up high before locking them in—the dancing lights were even brighter now, more active and more fluid. Once again she felt the call of the dance.

It was easier to ignore this time—her panic and concern for the boys overrode everything else as she repacked the trunk of the SUV with most of the stuff she'd taken out earlier, and added the camping stove and propane which she remembered just as she was heading out.

She turned for one last look at the cabin before leaving. She'd put out the candles, and now it was obvious that the building was lost to the infection—the aurora danced everywhere she looked, green and blue and yellow and gold, wafting like silk in a breeze. At the same time the drone started up again, a low hum at first but rising in volume quickly until it echoed and rang in her head.

"You want it? You're welcome to it," she muttered, and closed the door for the last time on her childhood.

31

Shaun's much anticipated big reunion with his family didn't go as he'd planned. He was driving through Melrose, just thankful that he'd survived almost three hours of hell on the road, when he was almost blinded by headlights coming in the other direction—full beam, not dipped.

He did what he always did in the situation, flicked the hi-beams of his vehicle off and on and pressed hard on the horn. The other car pulled up beside him.

"What the hell are you playing at?" he shouted as he wound his window down.

Becky stared back at him, open mouthed, her eyes wide.

"Never mind that. If you don't get rid of that cigarette right now, I'll ram it up your ass."

The boys wanted to get out of the car to greet him, and it broke Shaun's heart to have to order them to stay where they were.

He spoke to Becky through the rolled down windows.

"You okay?"

She nodded, tears rolling down her cheeks, and managed a smile.

"The cabin's gone though."

She didn't have to say any more—he'd seen more than enough of the infection by now to know just how voracious it could be.

"Don't get out—I'll turn around. Follow me up the road."

"Where are we going?"

"Bonavista, eventually —there's going to be a rescue boat up there tomorrow—I heard it on the radio. But for now I'd like to get inside somewhere and keep our heads down. I'm beat."

"Catalina? We should be able to find a shed or garage?"

"Okay—just give me a minute to turn round."

The feeling of relief he felt at finding them was almost overwhelming, but it was accompanied by a wash of tiredness, as if his mind and body were giving up, having accomplished their goal. He tried to concentrate on the road as he led them up and out of the village and along the short stretch of highway to the larger communities up the coast.

Judging by the lack of lights in the windows of the houses lining the highway, he didn't hold out much hope of finding anyone to help them. He'd heard many things on the radio on his drive up the peninsula—none of it good.

There had been more nukes deployed in the Korean crisis—many more nukes. The situation was, as with everything else, hazy at best, but Shaun didn't think there'd be much left in the Far East worth fighting over when all was said and done. Another war was raging in Iraq, most of Africa had gone quiet, as had South America, and the great cities of the West were being submerged under a tsunami tide of the fungus. Bypassing Toronto and Montreal on his way east had proved to be a smart move, as both cities were aflame, and attempts on the US Eastern Seaboard to deploy pesticides had only succeeded in poisoning much of the remaining population. The estimated death toll worldwide was now in the hundreds of millions, and still rising fast. One of the few talking heads remaining on air voiced a short phrase that now seemed to be on everyone's lips.

It's not a planet killer—it's a people killer.

He wasn't about to tell Becky any of this any time soon—just as he'd never speak of the drive up from Gander and the carnage he'd seen. There had been tall funeral pyres on the outskirts of Clarenville; an infected moose that was three quarters gone but still trying feebly to stay upright and a head-on collision that had killed three teenagers, a couple and their baby. Then there had been the weeping drip of greasy rot on the windshield all the way along the overhanging avenues.

Thankfully he could now put all that behind him, although

he was starting to feel the urge for a smoke. He fought it down—
Becky probably meant what she'd said at their meeting on the
road. Besides, the boat in Bonavista in the morning was now
taking precedence as the big thing to worry about—and first he
needed rest—and safety.

On entering Catalina past the Fish Processing plant, they
finally had a bit of luck. The forecourt of the auto repair shop
on the corner was empty—and the twin doors that led into
the building itself were partially open. Shaun pulled in, with
Becky's SUV coming up alongside. He wound the window
down again to speak.

"They've got concrete walls and floors, and a tin roof—we'll
be safe in there. I just need to get the doors open."

Becky nodded, and Shaun drove up as close as he could to
the partially open garage. He opened his door and rolled out,
going under the roll-up door and only standing when he was
sure he was fully inside. The only light was coming from the
headlights of their two vehicles, but the work area inside the
shop was empty and silent. He wasted no time in getting the
doors open and the two cars under the safety of the roof before
closing them in.

He got into the SUV with Becky and finally they had their
family reunion—tearful and almost hysterical such as it was.
Becky buried her head in his shoulder and sobbed, and the
boys leaned over from the back, arms wrapped around his neck
almost tight enough to strangle him.

He didn't mind one bit.

32

The *Sea Princess* left St. John's harbor just after midnight. Rohit and Irene sat with their backs to the bulkhead. They felt the slight jolt as the lines were cast off outside, then came the roll and swell that told them they were no longer tethered to the dock. The noise in the hold swelled to a roar as the main engines kicked in. There wasn't going to be much in the way of conversation for a while.

But at least we won't have to worry about the drone.

The last few days were already taking on the texture of a dream in his mind, as if he could not quite process the fact that everything he knew, everything he had worked for, had been taken, gone without even much of a fight. Ahead there was only uncertainty, but that was something he knew how to deal with—it was little different from the leap he'd taken as a nineteen-year-old when he landed in London to undertake his degree.

And this time, I have a companion.

Irene hadn't left his side since they boarded, hadn't taken her hand from his, and he realized something else: things would seem a lot worse if she wasn't there. He was even starting to drift into an almost comfortable sleep when he was nudged back awake. One of the suited figures stood over them.

"Mr. Patel?" the newcomer said, having to shout to be heard over the noise of the engines. "The Captain would like a word."

Rohit and Irene got to their feet.

"Just you, sir," the man said.

Rohit shook his head.

"Where I go, she goes."

The man didn't argue, and Irene gave Rohit's hand an extra squeeze as they followed the suited figure up the steep flight of metal stairs that led up and out of the hold.

The first thing Rohit noticed on the bridge was the relative quiet after the engine's boom in the hold. The second was the dark shape of the island off to the port side, and the swirling aurora of dancing rainbow lights that hung over the whole length of it.

"Don't look at it," someone said. "It tries to drag you in—it whispers in your brain."

"Another adaptation," Rohit said, almost to himself. "And just like the others, designed to trap prey."

"So they were right," someone else said, and Rohit turned to see a man—the captain at a guess—seated in a chair behind a bank of controls. "You are an expert?"

Rohit shrugged.

"As much as anyone is. I'm a mycologist, a fungi specialist if you like."

"Oh, I like," the captain replied. "Come on through. I've got coffee on the brew."

Still with Irene's hand in his, they went through to a small but tidy cabin at the rear of the bridge that seemed to serve as a tea room of sorts, although there were more than a few liquor bottles on the high shelf above the small stove. A music system that looked to be older than Rohit sat in the corner beneath a shelf of vinyl records.

The coffee was strong and piping hot, and did much to bring Rohit fully awake. And the captain seemed only to eager to bring them up to date on what was going on.

"We're heading for Labrador, eventually," he said. "We'll pick up as many survivors as we can, but I suspect it won't be many at all. Things are bad all over."

While they drank the coffee, they heard the same stories that Shaun had heard on his radio—mayhem and chaos, all across the planet.

"Will our plan to head for the cold work?" the Captain asked, and it took Rohit several seconds before he realized that the question had been aimed at him.

"It might," he finally replied. "It depends what, if any, homeothermic abilities were designed into the thing. Given how quickly it is showing us new adaptations though, I wouldn't put anything past it."

"What do you mean, designed?" the captain asked.

It was only then that Rohit discovered that his theory about the Chinese, and their experiments, was just that—his theory. No one else had joined the dots. He spent the next ten minutes laying it out for the captain, firstly to disbelief growing on disdain, then, finally, to a degree of acceptance as Rohit made the captain see the sense of his case.

"Does any of this actually help us any?"

Rohit didn't have an answer to that, until Irene nudged him in the ribs.

"You didn't tell him about the neuro-thingy … you know, the stuff that kills it?"

The captain, as it turned out, knew about the general effects of ethanol on the fungus, but yet again, the connection had not been made between that and the destruction of whatever control centers might be buried in the matrix of mycelia.

"Are you telling me that we can somehow systemically kill this thing off—like killing the roots of a weed to kill the foliage?" the captain asked.

"If we have enough toxin? Possibly."

It was currently a moot point anyway. They were far enough offshore to be away from much fear of infection now.

We're safe, for the time being.

33

Noble was somewhere deep in the forward hold that held the food and water supplies. As he walked among the crates and packages he slapped an exposed palm across the surfaces, drumming in time to the beat that pounded in his empty skull.

We have danced since before life walked on land, and we will dance long after there is nothing else but the black and the rock. We will dance in the black as the moon falls into our arms, and when the sun dims and goes dark we will dance on, into the stars, black on black, until the very end, when all is black, all is the dance.

We will dance.

Lost in the dark.

Lost in the dance.

34

Rebecca woke to see sunlight filtering in through the opaque windows of the garage doors. Despite the situation they had all fallen asleep, tiredness and relief washing them down to a place where worries could be forgotten, if only temporarily. She still couldn't quite believe that Shaun was there beside her but she was glad of his company, and glad that he took the driving duties in the SUV as they left the car shop and headed out into the day.

The infection had been busy while they were sleeping. The long pond opposite butted right up to the road, and every inch of its banks, and even across the shallower stretches of water, was infested with the fungal puffballs—each taller than a man and twice as broad. Just the sound of the SUV leaving the parking area triggered a bout of frantic activity. The nearest balls puffed and swelled, spewing out a dark cloud of spores that were taken high by an offshore wind, thankfully travelling away from the road and off into the brown, dead hillside to the west.

Shaun reached into his pocket—Rebecca knew that move only too well, he was going for a cigarette. She slapped at his hand.

"No way, mister. If you want one, you'll have to go outside."

That got her a smile that melted—for a second—the chills and worries that infested her, and as they made their way up through the deathly quiet of Catalina she started to think that they might yet get out of this alive. The feeling only lasted for a couple of hundred yards. When they got over the hill that led them along toward the center of the small town they saw twin plumes of smoke rising from the harbor ahead. As they got closer it was obvious that the fishing boats had been burned out—and not just the boats, but the Post Office, the small processing factory and Mifflins supermarket were all reduced to smoking husks. The car park outside Mifflins had also hosted a huge bonfire and they passed by just close enough to see the remains—bodies, scores of them, all burned rather than give them to the infection. The once neat houses that had lined the road for as long as Rebecca could remember were now buried under a matted swathe of filaments, and more puffballs stood up tall on roofs, like multiple chimneys, spouting spores in lieu of smoke.

The only movement was the spores and smoke swirling in the air and the swell and bloat of the puffballs that stood along the verges, as if providing an honor guard salute on the family's way out of the dead town.

The view did not improve any once they got out into the more open country at the far north end of the peninsula. What should be muddy pools and boggy moor was now a mass of brown tissue. The puffballs here, as if bloated by the damp, grew stronger and sturdier than ever, reaching taller than the stunted conifers around them that had been denuded and stripped to fuel the infection.

And everywhere she looked, Rebecca was aware of a subtle, but definitely present, aura, shimmering like an almost glimpsed rainbow at the skyline. There was also, faint and far off, the constant almost musical drone, and she felt her blood pounding in her ears in time. Shaun must have felt it too.

"Talk to me, Becky," he said. "Keep me in the here and now … and away from those Blue Hills."

For the next fifteen minutes she brought Shaun up to date with everything that happened, from her trip to the mall—and the pocket watch she still had in her purse—all the way through to the flight from the cabin. His eyes went wide when she spoke of the situation in St. John's.

"It's gone? It's all gone?"

She nodded, afraid to say any more, for if he started to cry, she'd join in, and neither of them might be able to stop. Shaun went quiet. When she finally asked him about how he'd got across country he looked grim.

"I caught a flight," was all he said. There was another long story there—she could read it in the set of his face and the sorrow in his eyes—but now wasn't the time to press him on it.

They went up the last long hill and Shaun stopped the SUV in the middle of the road as they looked down over the town of Bonavista—what was left of it. The infection and the associated puffballs were everywhere, an unbroken field of brown stretching down and away to the sea more than a mile away. It covered houses, service stations, the local college and the hockey stadium. More clouds of spores swirled in funnels like dust devils and, higher still, dark, wide fan-shapes glided and swooped in the wind. Even the tall water tower on the opposite hill had succumbed—it still had a blue bald dome on top, but the brown fungus would soon overrun that too. And once again, there was no sign of life apart from the fungus itself.

"We can't go down there," Rebecca whispered. "It's not safe."

Shaun looked grim again.

"I don't think it's safe anywhere, Becky. But there's a boat coming up from St. John's—it said so on the radio. And if it doesn't come, there'll be a boat or dinghy we can take for ourselves. If that happens, we're going to need more food and water, maybe enough to do us for a while. It's go down there … or nowhere."

The boys were quiet in the back—she hadn't heard the telltale click and thud of their games playing—and they were listening. She kept her voice calm as she replied.

"Down we go then."

"Once more into the valley of death," Shaun said.

He smiled, but she couldn't find one in reply.

At least the road itself was clear of infection, and when they reached the foot of the hill, the car park of the Foodlands store was flat and gray, fungus free. Shaun drew in to the middle of the lot and left the engine running.

"We need food and water—you agree?"

Rebecca nodded.

"But you can't go out there. There's too many spores in the air, it's too risky."

"It's the best we're going to do, There's nowhere in town with any shelter near the entrance, is there? I can get us to within a couple of feet of the door. It'll have to be enough."

She forced herself to think—but Shaun was right. Their current situation was as good as it got.

"You're right—but we all go. We're not splitting up again until this is over."

She didn't say the other words, but she knew they were both thinking them.

One way or the other.

"In that case," Shaun said grimly. "Let's do it properly."

Before Rebecca could comment he gunned the engine, floored the pedal and drove straight for the main picture window of the supermarket. They hit it at thirty, burst through in a shower of wood and shattered glass, and went almost four yards into the shop itself before being stopped beside the main tills.

"I always wanted to do that," Shaun said, and this time Rebecca did manage a smile in reply—a small one, but it was a start.

She made the boys get out the back window, for extra safety. They had to clamber and scramble over all the gear she had stowed in the trunk area, a task they seemed to enjoy, bringing more smiles from Shaun. Something that had been tight and restricting inside her for more than a day started to ease, a fraction. She checked that she'd be completely under cover, opened her door and stepped down to join the boys in the supermarket. Shaun left the engine running and stepped out to join them. The engine noise was enough to mask the droning hum that drifted in from beyond the parking lot.

"I'll get the water, you and the boys get food," Shaun said, but she stopped him before he left their side.

"I said, we do this together, or not at all. Besides, you'll just sneak a smoke in if I leave you alone for a second. Take a trolley, mister. We're going shopping."

It was only then that she took a look around the supermarket shelves. Any shopping they were going to do was going to be limited. There was no bread, no milk—little of anything fresh at all—although thankfully there seemed to be no sign of infection, in this part of the store at least. The power was off, so that meant that anything in the refrigerated sections wasn't going to much use either.

"Looks like it will be tins or nothing," Shaun said beside her. "There's no water in the dispenser, and the liquor store has been cleared out. Someone's beaten us to it."

In the end they found a box of beef stew—twenty-four cans—eight cans of beans, a box of bacon flavored chips and some carrots. They stowed it in the back of the SUV beside the rest of the stuff.

"A couple of weeks if we're lucky," Rebecca said. "Maybe less."

Shaun nodded.

"Let's check the storeroom out back. They might have missed something."

The four of them went together to the rear of the store and through into the gloom of an unlit storage area. Thin, watery sun came in through high skylights.

The first thing Rebecca noticed was the almost overpowering stench of rot.

Something had indeed been missed.

She tugged at Shaun's sleeve.

"Come away. There won't be anything we can use."

Shaun turned to look at her. At the same moment a deep droning hum rose up around them and the air swam in an aura of rainbow color. She felt her head go light and woozy, and saw double—Shaun's worried face, shouting at her, and, beyond that, Blue Hills, purple sky, and a song she wanted to join.

Something shifted in the far corner of the store, and stood, coming into view out of the shadows, man-shaped but not a man—it might have been once, for it wore a red survival suit, of the kind fishermen used at sea in these parts. But whatever was inside the suit had stopped being human quite some time ago.

Shaun pulled Rebecca away. She was vaguely aware that Mark was helping Shaun and trying to drag his younger brother out of the storeroom. Adam, like her, was answering a different call. There was something behind the man in the red suit. It seemed to be a huge mass of brown tissue in what looked very like a thick root system, stretched—embedded—across the far wall of the store. The roots grew from a central clump in the corner, a mass of ridged and crenellated tissue some six feet across from which tendrils, each as thick as a snake, wafted in the air, as if tasting, searching.

The song swelled and Rebecca knew that there was something in that central lump of tissue, something that recognized her—something that called to her, offering peace, calm, and no fear.

She saw the Blue Hills clearer than ever, heard the song, louder than ever.

She felt like dancing.

The next thing she knew Shaun had her by the shoulders and was screaming into her face. Her head cleared, slowly. She was leaning against the side of the SUV. Adam and Mark sat in the back. Adam looked as dazed as she felt.

"I said, get in the fucking car," Shaun yelled again, and this time she didn't need to be told again. She got into the passenger side and Shaun wasted no time. He got in the driver's seat, put his foot to the floor and they went out of the broken window in another shower of wood and glass.

As they turned to go out of the parking lot Rebecca took a look back.

A red-suited figure stood in the ruin of the window.

It still looked like a man—but there was only a ridged, crenellated ball of brown tissue where the head should be.

And somehow, he was still able to sing.

35

Dinosaurs living around 100 million years ago may have experienced acid trips after eating grass infected by a fungus similar to the species used to create LSD. Paleobiologists have discovered the earliest specimen of grass ever found trapped inside a piece of amber dug from a mine in the mountains of northern Myanmar. When they examined the grass, however, they found the tips were infected with a fungus that is thought to be similar to Ergot, a group of fungi that grow on rye and wheat.

There had been no one for the *Sea Princess* to pick up from Carbonear that morning. They arrived with the dawn, and stayed for an hour—and a bit longer—but all there was to be seen was puffballs and spores, swirling aurora of light and gliding, swooping fragments in the sky. The peninsula belonged to the fungus.

As the boat crossed the mouth of Trinity Bay heading for Bonavista, the clouds parted and the sun came out; ten miles from shore and they seemed to be clear of all effects of the infection although the dark, swirling heaviness still loomed above the western horizon. The captain allowed everyone a turn on deck to get some air.

Rohit, with Irene still holding tight to his hand, got his turn around ten o'clock, and it was only when he felt fresh air on his face and heard the squawk and cry of gulls overhead that he realized how oppressive the atmosphere in the hold had become.

He saw that the gulls were congregating on one spot on the

surface a few hundred yards ahead. He led Irene up to the prow to try to get a closer look. At first glance it looked like a whale feeding frenzy. Then he saw the infection. There was indeed a pod of whales near the surface—but the fungus had got them all, in large brown patches along the sides of the gaping mouths and running along the bodies, covering the tails. The huge animals floundered and thrashed at the surface, as if confused.

The gulls fed, tearing chunks of flesh and blubber from the whales' sides. Rohit saw more splashing, closer to the boat's hull. A school of dolphins swam alongside; at intervals they would come closer to the boat, then swim away quickly, keeping a distance.

As if there's something about the boat that scares them.

Then he heard it—the droning hum of the distant song, at the same time as his head started to float. He turned full circle to identify the source of the sound. It wasn't, as he had thought, coming from the dying whales, but from somewhere below his feet, somewhere on the boat.

A seagull overhead dropped a streak of fecal matter at his feet as he headed for the bridge to warn the captain. It was mostly white, but laced through with thin, brown, filaments.

He had to shake the captain, hard, to get his attention—the man seemed almost half-asleep, lost in a daze. Other members of the crew on the bridge seemed similarly afflicted, and Rohit felt Irene's hand slip from his as she too stared, unseeing, out the large window.

He had to work fast, for he felt the tug of the song in his head, and it was most persuasive. He went through to the small room at the back. After a bad moment when he thought there was no plug on the music system, but finally he found it, plugged it in, and got the turntable going. There was a record already on there, and he dropped the needle on it, not caring what it was, just needing the sound.

He turned the volume up to ten and the call of the infection immediately faded.

The *Sea Princess* made her way across Trinity Bay to the sound of a wailing heavy-metal band that Rohit didn't know.

But that didn't matter. He'd managed to mask the call of the song for now. But it was clear: the infection was aboard the boat—and they had to find it.

Before it spreads too far to be stopped.

The captain initially wanted to put Rohit and Irene back in the hold. Rohit fought against it, mainly because he knew that the call of the song would be louder there. He didn't tell the captain that—instead he argued from the basis of his knowledge and expertise, his ability to gauge the situation should the infection be found. In the end the man relented. Rohit suspected it was more that he grew tired of the argument rather than any merit of Rohit's techniques of persuasion. In any case, he, and Irene—she refused to be parted from his as vehemently as he had refused to go back in the hold—ended up below decks in a search team, following behind the hazmat-suited man, Kerry, who had spoken to them on their arrival. They all wore earplugs, and had to shout at each other to be heard, but it was better than the alternative.

Down below the song was louder, more insistent, and far away from the pounding metal band still playing on the bridge. Even through the earplugs Rohit felt its call, and he had taken to humming to himself, nonsense tunes he remembered from his childhood in India that seemed to help alleviate the pull of the infection's song.

They were headed for the forward hold. The captain had asked him where the infection was most likely to spread. Rohit had replied. "Anywhere it can feed." And the captain had gone white. Now here they were, less than five minutes later, approaching the storage hold where all the shipboard supplies were kept.

Rohit knew they were on the right track as they approached the closed door that led to the hold. A rainbow aurora, faint but unmistakable, hung in the air, a specter showing them the way to the feast.

36

"So, why weren't you affected, back in the store?" Becky said. They were parked on the old stone jetty in Bonavista harbor, facing out to sea. They'd been there for an hour now, with no sign of any boat, and they couldn't get anything on any radio station to tell them whether they still had hope of a rescue. They hadn't seen a single other living thing apart from the infection.

Shaun took a while to reply to her question—he didn't rightly know how to answer it. All he knew was that he'd almost lost her. In fact, she'd been so far gone that she'd fought and scratched at him as he dragged her away. She didn't seem to remember that part, and he wasn't about to tell her any time soon.

"I was affected, but I seemed to be able to fight it better than you could. Maybe it's the nicotine?" he said with a smile. It was worth a try—he'd only been back on the smokes for just over a day, and already he wanted another—the old addiction was hard to crack, doubly so after you'd slipped back into it.

She punched him on the shoulder, hard.

"Don't even think of it, buster. Besides, Mark was like you, and Adam was like me."

"Something in the genes then?" Shaun replied, voicing something he'd been thinking about for a while. "Maybe some folks have more natural immunity than others?"

Their conversations had been like this since they parked— going round in circles.

And without answers we'll just keep going round and round.

At least the view had improved; by parking to face the sea they were inured against the sight of the worst ravages of the infection. Dark clouds still roiled just overhead, but out toward the horizon all was blue and sparkling. That's where Shaun's hope lay, and he kept his eyes fixed on it, waiting for the first sign of a prow, a funnel—rescue.

Adam had fallen into a fitful sleep again in the back seat, curled up in a corner. Mark had leaned forward with his head poked through between the front seats and an arm draped over Shaun's shoulder, reassuring himself by touch that Shaun was still here.

I'll never leave them again.

That was something else he'd been thinking on for a while. Alberta had been all well and good—steady work and good money—but it had also almost cost him his family. The way the world was going he'd probably never have to make the decision again, but he made the promise to himself anyway.

I'll never leave them again.

Ten minutes later and without warning the SUV tilted with a lurch, the nose going down on Shaun's side.

"Puncture?" Becky asked.

"I don't think so. We're not moving, and a slow puncture would have been, well ... slow. This is something else."

He put a hand on the door handle, intending to step out and check, but Becky stopped him.

"Leave it," she said, softly. "It's too risky."

"But we might not be able to get going again if ..."

She put a hand on his arm.

"I know. Just leave it, okay? Either the boat comes, or it doesn't. Either way, we're not intending on driving anywhere, are we?"

They'd talked about what to do if the boat didn't arrive by dusk. From where they sat they could see three small cabin cruisers and a yacht tied up in the inner dock. The plan was to take one of them—anyone that had fuel. That plan too had its risks: they'd all have to brave the air outside for as long as it took to get aboard and loaded. They'd already decided to put that off as long as possible.

He took his hand from the door handle. Suddenly, more than ever, he wanted another smoke.

37

Irene's grip on his left hand was back as tight as ever, yet somehow comforting as Kerry opened the door to the cargo hold and went through first, with Rohit right behind, face almost pressed against the man's backpack. He smelled the ethanol. He'd smelled it all the way down, ever since standing next to the man when the spray-kit was filled. They were using a gardening tool normally used to moisten greenhouse plants, but from what Rohit had already seen it seemed to do the job admirably, the alcohol killing any fungus it touched. His main worry as he stepped into the hold was that they hadn't brought enough of it.

That worry was confirmed seconds later when Kerry stepped back, almost knocking Rohit over, then started spraying everywhere. Rohit saw the reason when the man moved slightly to one side—the whole cargo hold was infested. The rainbow aurora hung everywhere, and just looking at it made Rohit's head feel woozy again, so much so that he had to close his eyes momentarily to regain his composure.

"Back," he heard Kerry shout. "We have to go back."

"No!" Rohit shouted. "Hose it. Hose it all. We need to kill it."

"But the supplies …"

"They're gone. Hose it all down. And do it quick—can't you feel it?"

Rohit opened his eyes. The dancing light was seductive, and the whining hum could be heard too, even through the earplugs. Kerry hosed, sweeping the pistol grip left and right in wide arcs. The smell of ethanol became almost overpowering, but Rohit's head cleared and the drone of the fungus' song seemed to falter and fade.

"It's working," Irene shouted out.

A dark shape loomed out of the shadows, a man in a hazmat suit—but it wasn't reinforcements. The new arrival lumbered and stumbled as if drunk, almost falling into Kerry, but doing it with enough momentum to send them both rolling to the ground. It was only sheer luck that saved Kerry; he had the pistol grip in his hand as he threw a punch, and sent a spray of ethanol over the attacker, who rolled away and fell still, slumped against the bulkhead.

Kerry lay on the floor near the doorway, panting as if he'd just run a mile.

"My back's gone," he said, clearly in pain. "Get me out of here."

Rohit shook his head.

"Not yet. The job's not done."

He had Irene help him roll Kerry over—an operation accompanied by much swearing and yelps of pain, but enough to convince Rohit that the man wasn't too badly hurt and would live. They unstrapped the pack from his back, and Rohit put it on, tightening the straps to stop it slipping off again.

"He's right," Irene shouted, even while helping him with the buckles. "We really should get out of here."

"This won't take long," Rohit replied, and started to wash the place down with the alcohol, stepping farther into the gloom of the hold as he sprayed systematically across every crate and box.

The infection retreated before him as he went farther in, the brown filaments washing away with the alcohol, the dancing aurora dimming and flickering like a sputtering candle. The retreat seemed to be following a definite course, all the die-off proceeding backward towards a point in the far corner of the hold.

Is there a source?

Rohit kept walking. Irene did not hold his free hand, but she was there, just a yard behind him. He was washing a spray of fungus-killer to his left, and almost jerked in surprise when she called out.

"Rohit—on your right!"

He instinctively turned. The aura of light flared as the alcohol hit a tangled mass of brown tissue that was wedged in the corner of the hold. It looked more like a distorted tree trunk than any fungus, thick and bulbous, with root-like tendrils—some as thick as Rohit's thigh—stretching off and away along the walls, and the roof. The swell of the song grew louder still, and Rohit's earphones did little to mask it; the dancing light seemed to penetrate even through his eyelids, flickering inside his skull, promising calm, togetherness—if only he would put down the pistol grip and stop.

"Kill it. Kill it now." Irene shouted. "Before it gets us too."

Rohit's finger tightened on the trigger and he sent a wash of alcohol over the central mass of tissue. The whole organism, trunk and roots and all, jerked and went into a spasm as if struck. The drone turned to a screaming wail—loud, but one that held no hypnotic compulsion in it.

"Again," Irene shouted, and Rohit complied. The wash did not seem to be affecting the outer surface of the infection much, if at all—but the wailing whine cut off, leaving them in a gloomy, dark silence as the aurora flickered, then faded away completely.

They did not have time to contemplate their seeming victory. Even as the main body of the fungus went still and quiet, Kerry shouted from across the hold.

"Get over here. He's still moving."

The thing that had attacked Kerry had once been a man—indeed, it seemed he was known.

"My God, it's Jim Noble."

"How can you tell?" Irene asked, just before Rohit said the same thing. The body on the ground seemed to have swollen and bloated inside the hazmat suit, making the material look tight and stretched much wider than its normal girth. The fact there had been a man inside was obvious from the single blue eye, patch of hair and an ear visible on the left-hand side. But the rest of the head was covered in a tight mat of the brown infection, and had already hardened to become almost woody across the whole right hemisphere of the skull.

And it was definitely still alive. It crawled, on all fours, heading in a straight line for the dark corner containing the thick mass of tissue.

"Spray it. Kill it." Kerry shouted. The man's back seemed to have improved remarkably, for he stood, and was backing away quickly toward the doorway.

Rohit shook his head.

"Let's see what's happening. We might learn something."

"Yes. And we might get dead. You do what you like. I'm out of here."

Kerry left Rohit and Irene alone in the hold, and would have shut them in had Irene not stepped into the doorway.

"I'll get the captain," Kerry shouted as he left.

Rohit knew that the captain's first instinct would be to slash and burn. If he was to learn anything, it had to be now.

The crawling figure seemed to be ignoring them completely. Once they were sure Kerry was actually gone and would not be returning to seal them in, Rohit and Irene followed across the floor of the hold.

It headed straight for the corner. Six feet from the woody mass it reached the first of the thicker roots. The thing in the suit put out a hand, and even before it touched the root a blue and green shimmer passed across the gap in the air, some six inches off the floor. The humming drone started again, almost too faint to hear, but getting louder as the shimmer brightened, passing from the hazmat suit across to the roots and dancing up the tendril toward the main body which seemed to quiver, as if in anticipation.

It's communicating. More than that—it's replenishing itself.

He had a flash of inspiration.

They're both memory nodes, the suited thing and the woody mass—and they can talk to each other, maybe even heal each other.

"Hose it again," Irene said. "It's getting stronger. I can feel it."

She was right. He had got noticeably light-headed just in the last few seconds and the dancing aura of color had strengthened. He sprayed the woody mass again, and the shimmering— and the humming—faded. He also noticed that he no longer felt the weight of the pack on his back, and when he moved he didn't get the side-to-side sloshing sensation that had been there minutes before.

I'm almost out of juice.

The suited figure crawled forward again, still making for the main mass in the corner.

"Hose it—hose it now," Irene shouted.

"And if you don't, I will," another voice said. The captain had joined them, and he wore a backpack of his own. Behind him were two men carrying cans of kerosene.

"Wait," Rohit said. "I might have an idea. We need this one alive."

38

Noble came reluctantly out of the dance, out of the black and into the light once more. It hurt—lancing into his eyes, his skull, seeming to penetrate all the way through to his bones.

Something ate into him, something that was inside, something that had joined the dance. He wanted to scream at the searing, blistering pain of it but his mouth wouldn't respond, his limbs wouldn't move. Molten fire, like lava, ran through his veins, threatening to consume him utterly.

He stopped dancing, lost his partners; lost the song.

"It's working," a voice said, far, far away.

Then there was just the pain—endless, white-hot pain.

39

Rebecca almost wept with joy just after noon when they got their first sighting of the red keel of the approaching supply vessel; it came slowly into view around the headland that bounded the eastern side of the harbor. Shaun flashed the SUV's headlights, half a dozen times, and they all heard the answering blasts of the boat's horn, even above the noise of the car engine.

She wasn't worried when her side of the car dipped suddenly—whatever had caused the axle to give way on Shaun's side seemed to be spreading.

But the cavalry's here. We're saved.

She thought that the boat might stop offshore and send a tender or dinghy in to the small harbor, but it kept coming until it loomed large in the windshield, and docked just thirty yards ahead of them up the jetty. She now saw that it wasn't just a supply boat—it also had a ferry deck, and was already lowering a ramp to allow them access.

"Can we move?" she asked Shaun.

"Only one way to find out."

Shaun released the brake and put his foot on the pedal. Something squealed in a high whine, the engine coughed, twice, then gave in with a rumble that indicated it was badly busted up in there. The engine knocked and sputtered. It was still running, but not delivering any power to the wheels. Wisps of black smoke rose from under the hood. Shaun kept pumping the pedal but it was obvious they weren't going anywhere.

Shaun flicked the headlights several times. They heard an amplified voice call out, though they couldn't make out the words until Rebecca gingerly wound her window down slightly. "Stay put. We're coming to you."

The next five minutes went past excruciatingly slowly—for the first two of them there seemed to be no activity at all—then three people in full hazmat gear, all wearing backpacks, could be seen on the high viewing area outside the bridge windows. They descended a ladder, going out of sight, and that was that for another couple of minutes until, finally, they heard the roar of a large engine and a truck came up out of the ferry deck, coming along the jetty toward them. It stopped just inches from their fender and the three suited figures got out.

Rebecca started to wind down the window, planning to talk to them, when Shaun held her back.

"Wait. Something's up."

The suited figures looked closely at the front tires for several seconds, then stood back to allow one of them access. He washed a spray over the whole front and sides of the SUV, and Rebecca smelled it oozing through the gaps in the bodywork and up from the floor—an almost overpowering whiff of alcohol and, beneath that, the faintest hint of disinfectant.

It was only when they were satisfied that one of the suited figures approached her window and tapped on it, indicating she should roll it down.

"Please step out," a male voice said. The voice came from behind a mask that hid most of his features. "One at a time. We'll take this slow."

Shaun went first. They hosed him down, head to toe, and he was still dripping when Mark went out on the same side to join him. Rebecca turned to Adam. The boy was still curled up in the back corner. He looked asleep, but something lurched in her heart as she leaned over and reached for him.

She didn't quite manage it—one of the suited figures pulled open her passenger door and dragged her bodily from the vehicle. She screamed even as she was hosed down.

"Adam!"

The boy didn't reply. He didn't open his eyes, didn't seem quite awake, but Rebecca had seen enough to know what the problem was—thin brown filaments ran from the SUV's trunk, around the corner of the back seat, and across the skin of the boy's neck.

Adam was infected.

40

"Where's my son. I want to see my son."

Rohit heard the man shouting even through the metal door of the small room that served as the boat's medical center. He'd had the lad brought straight in—hosing him down hadn't got to the infection in time; it was inside him.

But there was hope.

He had two bodies laid out on tables in the room—the lad, and the clean-up worker, Noble. Rohit's idea had indeed worked. After bringing Noble up out of the cargo hold, they'd injected him with a dilute dose of ethanol, and waited. It had taken two hours, and the man wasn't out of the woods yet by any means, but the infection had definitely retreated. He still had a fist-sized lump of foreign tissue, like a goiter, at the junction of his neck and shoulder. Rohit suspected that this was the nerve system—the small brain—of the thing. It had him worried.

"Let the family in," Rohit said to Irene, who hadn't left his side this whole time. "We need to ask their permission."

"Permission for what?" Irene asked.

"Permission to inject the boy. It might be his only chance."

"Can I hold him?" the mother—Becky, her husband said—asked.

Rohit shook his head.

"It's not safe. And even after the injection, if you agree to it, he will have to be kept isolated for a while—just to be safe."

"But the injection will work?" the husband asked. He hadn't taken his eyes of the boy, and tears weren't far from the surface.

"It worked on Noble—at least partially," Rohit replied, and motioned at the other prone man.

It was only then that the wife paid attention to the other body.

"Shaun, look. He's like that one in the supermarket, where we saw those roots."

Now it was Rohit's turn to pay attention.

"If you've seen this before—and the roots—I'll need to know everything. But first, do I have your permission for the injection?"

The couple looked at other, and the husband nodded. Rohit injected a seven per cent solution into the boy's arm. The boy's eyelids fluttered but there was no other movement.

"What now?" Becky asked.

"Now we wait. I'll have some coffee brought through and you can tell me everything."

The captain planned to cast off and get going on the next tide. Rohit realized that he might have to ask for more time after hearing the family's story. He went to the bridge to try to explain his thinking. Yet again, Irene followed at his side. The family stayed with their lad. He still hadn't shown any signs of movement, but the infection had not spread any further in the last fifteen minutes, so there was hope yet.

"It's using people as carriers for the … brains … for want of a better word," Rohit said to the captain. "Noble brought a nerve cluster on board with him and it spread into the hold—you've seen the root system and the … brain. That's how it spreads, at least that's how it spreads the part of it that knows how to react and adapt. If we can stop that, then the rest of it is just tissue— the rest of it can be eradicated."

The captain looked as tired as any man he'd ever seen.

"And can you stop it? Do you have a plan?"

"I do. But you're not going to like it. I want to try to wake Noble up, then press gang him into something that'll probably kill him."

41

The pain had faded now, leaving behind a dull ache. Everything seemed flat and colorless. There was no song, no dancing, and Noble missed them—needed them, a junkie needing his fix. His body felt as if ants crawled all over it, but he couldn't move to scratch. A face loomed over his—dark skinned, Asian—he didn't recognize the man, and had to struggle to remember how to make sense of what was being said.

"Can you hear me, Mr. Noble?"

Noble struggled, couldn't find speech; his chest and throat felt too solid, like rock, refusing to move to his command. He managed to move his head, a single small nod, but it seemed to please the man speaking to him.

"We think we've found a way to stop it spreading," the man said. "But we need your help. We're going to inject you with more of the toxin, as it has successfully brought you back this far. But this will be a bigger dose. We want you to go back down onto the hold and make contact with the thing you left there— we want you to poison it. Understand, this may kill you, but the infection has riddled you already, and either way, you don't have much time. Nod again if you agree."

Noble understood none of it apart from one thing—they wanted to put him back in the dark, back with the dance.

There was nothing he'd like more.

He nodded.

42

Shaun couldn't take it anymore. The sight of Adam lying on the trestle, as helpless as the day he'd been born, was too much to bear. When the doctor, Rohit, said he was going down to the hold to see if his theory was right—if there was a way to stop the infection in its tracks—Shaun volunteered to go and help, if he could.

Becky was furious, at first.

"We said it, didn't we ... we'd never be parted again."

"And I meant it," he replied. "I'll be right below here—just a flight of stairs away—and I'm not about to do anything stupid. I'm all out of stupid. Besides, it might help Adam."

She punched him on the shoulder, hard, and he knew she would let him go, for she understood better than anyone how much it was tearing him up to just stand around doing nothing while Adam lay there.

Rohit administered an injection to the man on the other table. Shaun didn't really understand what was going on—only that the man, badly infected, had volunteered to take a poison, and then to deliver it to something in the hold, something that Shaun thought might be the same as the thing he'd seen in the supermarket.

I managed to fight it then—I might be of help in fighting it now.

When Rohit asked for help in getting Noble down to the hold, Shaun went to his side.

"Wash your skin with the alcohol," Rohit said. "It'll stop you being infected."

"Maybe I should have a smoke too?" Shaun replied, with a smile for Becky's benefit. Rohit surprised him by taking the suggestion seriously.

"You may be on to something there," the doctor replied. "Nicotine, in concentration, is known to be effective as a neuro-toxin. In fact, it might work even better than the ethanol. When we have a chance, I must test that too. But first, let's get Noble downstairs. If this works, it'll be our first bit of good news. I think we could all use some."

Shaun swabbed his hands and face with ethanol. The smell of it brought about an instinctive craving for a smoke that he had to push down.

Smokes and booze are a hell of a way to go about saving the world.

On the way down below, Shaun braced himself for a return of the light-headedness, listening for the swell of the droning song, watching out for the flicker and dance of the rainbow aurora. But there was nothing, just the clomp of their footsteps on the decks. He had Noble's left side, Rohit was on the right and the other woman, Irene, just behind them. She wore one of the backpacks, and Shaun saw her knuckles whiten where she gripped the pistol trigger.

Rohit stopped at a door, the entrance to the hold.

"If this doesn't work, we need to get out fast. If I say run, you run. No heroics."

Shaun almost laughed.

"I guarantee you, doc—I'll be first out."

Rohit smiled back, then led them into the gloom of the hold. The whole place stank of alcohol. There were crates and boxes of food piled high, but all seemed ruined, infested with black slime that was what remained of the perished mycelia. The thing they had come for—the thing they wanted to reintroduce Noble too—was lodged in the far corner. It was a thick, woody mass of tissue.

"It is the same," Shaun whispered, then spoke up louder so Rohit could hear him. "It's the same as the thing in the supermarket."

Rohit nodded.

"If I'm right, these are the brains—the control centers if you like—of the infestation. Let's see if we can level the field and make it stupid."

As they approached the mass of roots Noble grew more animated and pulled against Shaun's grip, seemingly eager to approach the corner.

"Let him go," Rohit said. "This is why we came."

Shaun and Rohit both let go of Noble and stepped back to stand alongside Irene, who kept the spray gun trained on the man's back as he half-walked, half-stumbled into the corner of the hold, falling onto the mass of brown trunk and root.

Almost immediately the drone started, and dancing lights in blue and green rose from Noble's body. He started to tear at his hazmat suit, ripping it off. The colors flowed out of him, around him, and across the divide, seeping into the body of the root system. Irene stepped forward and raised the spray gun, but Rohit held her back.

"Wait, we need to see what happens."

Shaun felt slightly woozy, but no worse than if he'd had a few beers. The droning song stayed low, far off, and he felt no compulsion to step closer to the rainbow aurora. Noble went still and quiet; his body inside the suit collapsed in on itself with a moist gurgle, and black fluid leaked onto the trunk and root. The main body of the infection reacted immediately, bubbling and seething, like vinegar on baking soda. The reaction spread quickly, through the trunk and along the root system, sending a stench of rot so strong that the three of them were forced to step back, all the way to the door of the hold.

43

The dark and the dance called.
Noble went to it, gladly.

44

"Well, that seemed to work," Irene said. She lowered the spray gun and took Rohit's hand. "You were right."

Rohit went back into the depths of the hold, walked over and looked down at what was left of Noble. It wasn't pretty, just a corroded mass of dark, moist tissue that was still bubbling. The drone faded and died, and the last of the dancing lights sputtered, flared briefly, then faded completely. The stench didn't fade though, and was bad enough that they had to back out of the hold.

The captain stood on the other side of the doorway.

"Now what?" he said, and Rohit saw that yet again, the question had been aimed at him.

"Now we adapt," Rohit said. "I want to see if it works out in the wild. I need to go to that supermarket."

Any further discussion was halted by a shout from above—the woman, Becky.

"Doctor, come quick."

Her husband was first to reach the Medical Room but Rohit wasn't far behind.

The boy was worse than ever. Brown filaments drew thin lines across his cheeks and over his hands and his breathing was coming fast and panting, his chest heaving as if under immense pressure.

"Do something, Doc," Becky shouted. "Save my boy."

Rohit turned to the captain, who stood in the doorway.

"I need to go to where these folks saw the other one. He's linked to the place of infection—I think that's how this stuff works. If we kill the nodes, we kill all the infection in that area."

"I can't ask anyone to go back out there," the Captain said. "It's too dangerous."

"And it's not your son," Becky replied. She stepped forward. "Tell us what you need, Doc. Just do it quick, for I'm getting my boy back, one way or the other."

Ten minutes later they were in the truck—Rohit, Irene and the family all crammed in up front. Becky had the stricken lad in her lap; they'd got the boy into full hazmat gear and mask, containing the infection inside.

I hope.

Shaun drove while Rohit held Irene's hand in his left, carrying a large syringe containing a concentrated dose of ethanol in his right.

"What's the plan, Doc?" Shaun said.

"We find the man you saw in the survival suit, we inject him with this, and we introduce him back to the nerve cluster. It'll probably kill him, but I can't think of another option right now."

"And then?"

"And then we hope. If it works, then all the infection controlled by that cluster should die back and rot. If that's the case, we tell the world, and start adapting to the new way of things— we fight back."

"And if it doesn't work? Becky asked.

This time it was Irene that answered.

"Then we're all fucked."

It was obvious as they made their way up Church Street that the fungus was now in complete control. Every building was little more than a mound of filaments—siding or roof peeking through in places to show what was underneath, what was being consumed. Tall puffballs, some as high as the eaves of the buildings, filled all the spaces that had once been green vegetation, all crammed together tightly, like ranked pins in a surreal bowling alley.

The noise of the truck was enough to bring a flurry of activity—as they passed the puffballs swelled and contracted, sending out dense clouds of spore that rattled like hail on the hood and roof of the truck. As they went down the incline out of the main part of town towards the Foodlands forecourt some of the fungus detached from its hold on the ground and rolled with them. They drove downhill accompanied by a score or more of the rough balls, one of which went under the wheels. The truck squashed it without a bump, but it got Rohit thinking of the way the family's SUV had got infected in the first place—into the tires and up the wheel arches. If his plan didn't work, they might all be infected before they got back to the boat.

It was starting to feel more and more like a last throw of the dice.

That feeling got even stronger as they rolled into the Foodlands forecourt. Rohit didn't need the family to tell him that they'd found their man; a red suited figure lay, face down, on the concrete. He wasn't going to be going anywhere—a two-foot high puffball grew up proudly out of his back, and spurted a spray of spores over the truck as they pulled up at the wrecked window of the forecourt.

"What now?" Shaun asked.

Becky laughed bitterly.

"I think Irene got it right earlier."

Rohit looked out of the window, into the store. He could see some of the root system, even from here.

"We need an infected person."

He saw Becky instinctively pull her boy closer to her.

"You can't have him," Shaun said.

"That wasn't my plan at all," Rohit said, and before he could talk himself out of it, he let go of Irene's hand, opened the truck door, stepped out and over to the puffball, and gave it a kick.

Spores filled the air around him.

He breathed deeply.

45

"What in blazes did you do that for?" Shaun shouted from inside the truck. He felt like giving the doctor a good shaking, but as he'd said earlier, he was all out of stupid. There were too many spores in the air out there—anyone in them was just giving themselves a death sentence—and he'd promised Becky they wouldn't be parted again.

The droning hum started up again and Shaun's head spun.

"Shut the door, quickly now," Rohit said. He held up the syringe. "In two minutes I'll give myself this, and walk inside to say hello. If it works, all infection in the area will die when the node dies, and your boy should recover. If it doesn't work …"

Irene spoke first.

"I told you that one already," she said, and she too stepped out of the truck, closing the door behind her before going to join Rohit. The drone lessened, and Shaun's head cleared almost immediately. Irene gave the puffball another kick, and took a deep breath even as Rohit clasped her hand. The doctor injected himself at the wrist with half the contents of the syringe—Shaun saw him grimace and wince at the sudden pain before he got it under control. Irene put her arm out to be injected, and afterwards Rohit held her as tears ran down her cheeks.

The pair embraced for a long time before parting. With one last wave goodbye, they turned and headed into the store, still hand in hand.

46

"Do you feel it?" Irene said as they stepped through the broken and smashed front window.

Rohit nodded. His head floated, the beat of the song pounding in his empty skull. Inside the store brown filaments coated all of the stacks, giving it the appearance of a hedge-maze in winter. Light danced everywhere he looked; blues and greens and yellows and gold, cavorting in time to a beat that even now called Rohit onward, into the dark, into the dance.

"You're sure about this?" he said to Irene, hearing his voice echo, far off, as if spoken by someone else. She didn't speak, just gripped his hand tighter as they walked among the shelves.

His vision doubled, and he saw Blue Hills and a high plain. Tall puffballs—impossibly high—through dense clouds of spores upward, clouds that writhed and spun in rainbow spirals and whorls; clouds that danced.

Fire burned inside him, white flame and heat, coursing through him.

The toxin—it's working.

That was his last coherent thought.

They walked out of the maze of shelves and into the storeroom beyond. A bulbous woody thing, twenty feet across at least, waited for them in there—it also sat on the high plain between the Blue Hills. Rohit saw that its roots intertwined with others of its kind, a vast network that stretched into and through everything, a network that sang and danced and glowed in a rainbow arching high, filling the sky with the dance. It was beautiful.

Hand in hand, what was left of Rohit and Irene went together into the dark, dancing.

"I've got to go to help them," Shaun said. "I couldn't live with myself if I didn't."

Rebecca looked up at him.

"I know. I think it's too late for all of us anyway—I think this might be the end of the road."

"I love you," Shaun said.

She smiled back at him as Mark leaned over to join them in a family embrace.

"I know that too," she said, unable to see Shaun through her tears.

He opened the truck door.

There was no drone, no sound at all save the thin whistle of a rising breeze. Rebecca wiped her eyes clear and looked through the ruin of the window into the store, just in time to see a flash of brightness, a spectrum of swirling color that faded as the sun came out.

The brown filament that coated the shelving went dark, then black, dripping to the floor in oily clumps.

The puffball that grew from the back of the red suited man fell in on itself with a moist plop.

The stench of rot filled the air, even as bubbling black goop spilled from the store. Shaun climbed back inside and closed the door, thankfully masking the worst of the smell. Across the lot a row of tall puffballs gave out one last belch then collapsed inward, bubbling and suppurating until all that was left was more of the black rot.

Adam stirred in Rebecca's arms. His hand came up and he tore off his mask in order to take a deep breath. The brown

---

filaments on his face went black, then gray, then faded away completely.

"I was dreaming, mum. Blue Hills and a long valley—but it's all dead now. Are we home yet?"

Fresh tears filled her eyes as she pressed the boy close to her.

They sat there for long minutes as the infection failed and died around them, but no one ever came out of the store.

"So what now?" she asked.

It was almost an hour later as they went back down Church Street toward the harbor. There was no sign of brown—just oozing, black rot and collapsing puffballs. A rising wind was already blowing away the remnants of the looming clouds and the warmth of the sun seemed to be accelerating the rate at which the fungus fell in on itself.

"Is it over?" she said again.

"I don't think so. If the doc was right, we just killed this node and the bits of the infection that it controlled up this end of the peninsula. But we know how to do it now. They didn't die in vain."

They rounded the last corner and the boat came in sight, still sitting on the dock.

"So what do we do?" she asked again.

"We do what that stuff does—only better," Shaun replied. "We take territory, we adapt, we survive."

Shaun flashed his headlights half a dozen times, and the vessel's horn honked back at them. It sounded joyous, almost triumphant.

ABOUT THE AUTHOR

William Meikle is a Scottish writer, now living in Canada, with over twenty novels published in the genre press and more than 300 short story credits in thirteen countries. He has books available from a variety of publishers and his work has appeared in a large number of professional anthologies and magazines. He lives in Newfoundland with whales, bald eagles and icebergs for company. When he's not writing he drinks beer, plays guitar, and dreams of fortune and glory.

Curious about other Crossroad Press books?
Stop by our site:
http://store.crossroadpress.com
We offer quality writing
in digital, audio, and print formats.

Enter the code FIRSTBOOK
to get 20% off your first order from our store!
Stop by today!

55844448R00106

Made in the USA
Middletown, DE
18 July 2019